Acclaim for MARTIN McDONAGH's

The Beauty Queen of Leenane

"Stunning . . . McDonagh . . . has a master's hand at building up and subverting expectations in a cat-and-mouse game with the audience."
—*The New York Times*

"Bleakly amusing, violently lyric."
—*Newsday*

"Brilliant, dark and very funny. . . . What makes it so universally resonant is that McDonagh harnesses into a rich but moving comedy. The dialogue is so superbly shaped, the storytelling so skilled, that he absorbs the reader and fascination of a scary tale."
—*Daily News*

"Dazzlingly theatrical . . . full of unexpected twists."
—*USA Today*

"The Beauty Queen of Leenane is the darkest, most chillingly constructed, most assured play in years—and it's also one of the saddest and sweetest . . . an ebullient verbal jazz, part Samuel Beckett, part Honeymooners."
—*The Wall Street Journal*

"Painful and heart-rending . . . as fresh as it is harrowing. Scene after scene unfolds with flawless pace, a level of tension and menace simmering just below the surface."
—*Variety*

Also by MARTIN MCDONAGH

The Cripple of Inishmaan

The Beauty Queen of Leenane

AND OTHER PLAYS

MARTIN McDONAGH

The Beauty Queen of Leenane

AND OTHER PLAYS

VINTAGE INTERNATIONAL
Vintage Books
A Division of Random House, Inc.
New York

A VINTAGE INTERNATIONAL ORIGINAL, FIRST EDITION,
SEPTEMBER 1998

ISBN 0-375-70487-6

Contents

The Beauty Queen of Leenane   1

A Skull in Connemara   85

The Lonesome West   167

The Beauty Queen of Leenane

The Beauty Queen of Leenane, a Druid Theatre Company/Royal Court Theatre co-production, was first presented at the Town Hall Theatre, Galway, on February 1, 1996, marking the official opening of the theatre, and subsequently opened at the Royal Court Theatre Upstairs on March 5, 1996. This production was first presented in the United States at the Atlantic Theatre Co., New York, on February 26, 1998, and subsequently opened at the Walter Kerr Theatre, New York, on April 23, 1998. The cast was as follows:

MAG FOLAN	Anna Manahan
MAUREEN FOLAN	Marie Mullen
RAY DOOLEY	Tom Murphy
PATO DOOLEY	Brian F. O'Byrne

Directed by Garry Hynes
Designed by Francis O'Connor
Lighting designed by Ben Ormerod
Sound by David Murphy

CHARACTERS

MAUREEN FOLAN, *aged forty. Plain, slim.*
MAG FOLAN, *her mother, aged seventy. Stout, frail.*
PATO DOOLEY, *a good-looking local man, aged about forty.*
RAY DOOLEY, *his brother, aged twenty.*

Setting: Leenane, a small town in Connemara, County Galway.

– –

SCENE ONE

The living-room/kitchen of a rural cottage in the west of Ireland. Front door stage left, a long black range along the back wall with a box of turf beside it and a rocking-chair on its right. On the kitchen side of the set is a door in the back wall leading off to an unseen hallway, and a newer oven, a sink and some cupboards curving around the right wall. There is a window with an inner ledge above the sink in the right wall looking out onto fields, a dinner table with two chairs just right of centre, a small TV down left, an electric kettle and a radio on one of the kitchen cupboards, a crucifix and a framed picture of John and Robert Kennedy on the wall above the range, a heavy black poker beside the range, and a touristy-looking embroidered tea-towel hanging further along the back wall, bearing the inscription 'May you be half an hour in Heaven afore the Devil knows you're dead'. As the play begins it is raining quite heavily. MAG FOLAN, *a stoutish woman in her early seventies with short, tightly permed grey hair and a mouth that gapes slightly, is sitting in the rocking-chair, staring off into space. Her left hand is somewhat more shrivelled and red than her right. The*

3

front door opens and her daughter, MAUREEN, *a plain, slim woman of forty, enters carrying shopping and goes through to the kitchen.*

MAG: Wet, Maureen?

MAUREEN: Of course wet.

MAG: Oh-h.

MAUREEN *takes her coat off, sighing, and starts putting the shopping away.*

MAG: I did take me Complan.

MAUREEN: So you *can* get it yourself so.

MAG: I can. *(Pause.)* Although lumpy it was, Maureen.

MAUREEN: Well, can I help lumpy?

MAG: No.

MAUREEN: Write to the Complan people so, if it's lumpy.

MAG *(pause)*: You do make me Complan nice and smooth. *(Pause.)* Not a lump at all, nor the comrade of a lump.

MAUREEN: You don't give it a good enough stir is what you don't do.

MAG: I gave it a good enough stir and there was still lumps.

MAUREEN: You probably pour the water in too fast so. What it says on the box, you're supposed to ease it in.

MAG: Mm.

MAUREEN: That's where you do go wrong. Have another go tonight for yourself and you'll see.

4

MAG: Mm. (*Pause.*) And the hot water too I do be scared of. Scared I may scould meself.

MAUREEN *gives her a slight look.*

MAG: I *do* be scared, Maureen. I be scared what if me hand shook and I was to pour it over me hand. And with you at Mary Pender's, then where would I be?

MAUREEN: You're just a hypochondriac is what you are.

MAG: I'd be lying on the floor and I'm not a hypochondriac.

MAUREEN: You are too and everybody knows that you are. Full well.

MAG: Don't I have a urine infection if I'm such a hypochondriac?

MAUREEN: I can't see how a urine infection prevents you pouring a mug of Complan or tidying up the house a bit when I'm away. It wouldn't kill you.

MAG (*pause*): Me bad back.

MAUREEN: Your bad back.

MAG: And me bad hand. (MAG *holds up her shrivelled hand for a second.*)

MAUREEN (*quietly*): Feck . . . (*Irritated.*) I'll get your Complan so if it's such a big job! From now and 'til doomsday! The one thing I ask you to do. Do you see Annette or Margo coming pouring your Complan or buying your oul cod in butter sauce for the week?

MAG: No.

5

MAUREEN: No is right, you don't. And carrying it up that hill. And still I'm not appreciated.

MAG: You *are* appreciated, Maureen.

MAUREEN: I'm not appreciated.

MAG: I'll give me Complan another go so, and give it a good stir for meself.

MAUREEN: Ah, forget your Complan. I'm expected to do everything else, I suppose that one on top of it won't hurt. Just a . . . just a blessed fecking skivvy is all I'm thought of!

MAG: You're not, Maureen.

MAUREEN *slams a couple of cupboard doors after finishing with the shopping and sits at the table, after dragging its chair back loudly. Pause.*

MAG: Me porridge, Maureen, I haven't had, will you be getting? No, in a minute, Maureen, have a rest for yourself . . .

But MAUREEN *has already jumped up, stomped angrily back to the kitchen and started preparing the porridge as noisily as she can. Pause.*

MAG: Will we have the radio on for ourselves?

MAUREEN *bangs an angry finger at the radio's 'on' switch. It takes a couple of swipes before it comes on loudly, through static—a nasally male voice singing in Gaelic. Pause.*

MAG: The dedication Annette and Margo sent we still haven't heard. I wonder what's keeping it?

MAUREEN: If they sent a dedication at all. They only said they did. (MAUREEN *sniffs the sink a little, then turns to* MAG.) Is there a smell off this sink now, I'm wondering.

MAG (*defensively*): No.

MAUREEN: I hope there's not, now.

MAG: No smell at all is there, Maureen. I do promise, now.

MAUREEN *returns to the porridge. Pause.*

MAG: Is the radio a biteen loud there, Maureen?

MAUREEN: A biteen loud, is it?

MAUREEN *swipes angrily at the radio again, turning it off. Pause.*

MAG: Nothing on it, anyways. An oul fella singing nonsense.

MAUREEN: Isn't it you wanted it set for that oul station?

MAG: Only for Ceilidh Time and for whatyoucall.

MAUREEN: It's too late to go complaining now.

MAG: Not for nonsense did I want it set.

MAUREEN (*pause*): It isn't nonsense anyways. Isn't it Irish?

MAG: It sounds like nonsense to me. Why can't they just speak English like everybody?

MAUREEN: Why should they speak English?

MAG: To know what they're saying.

MAUREEN: What country are you living in?

MAG: Eh?

MAUREEN: What country are you living in?

MAG: Galway.

MAUREEN: Not what county!

MAG: Oh-h . . .

MAUREEN: Ireland you're living in!

MAG: *Ireland.*

MAUREEN: So why should you be speaking English in Ireland?

MAG: I don't know why.

MAUREEN: It's Irish you should be speaking in Ireland.

MAG: It is.

MAUREEN: Eh?

MAG: Eh?

MAUREEN: 'Speaking English in Ireland.'

MAG (*pause*): Except where would Irish get you going for a job in England? Nowhere.

MAUREEN: Well, isn't that the crux of the matter?

MAG: Is it, Maureen?

MAUREEN: If it wasn't for the English stealing our language, and our land, and our God-knows-what, wouldn't it be we wouldn't need to go over there begging for jobs and for handouts?

MAG: I suppose that's the crux of the matter.

MAUREEN: It *is* the crux of the matter.

MAG (*pause*): Except America, too.

MAUREEN: What except America too?

MAG: If it was to America you had to go begging for hand-outs, it isn't Irish would be any good to you. It would be English!

MAUREEN: Isn't that the same crux of the same matter?

MAG: I don't know if it is or it isn't.

MAUREEN: Bringing up kids to think all they'll ever be good for is begging handouts from the English and the Yanks. That's the selfsame crux.

MAG: I suppose.

MAUREEN: Of course you suppose, because it's true.

MAG (*pause*): If I had to go begging for handouts anywhere, I'd rather beg for them in America than in England, because in America it does be more sunny any-ways. (*Pause.*) Or is that just something they say, that the weather is more sunny, Maureen? Or is that a lie, now?

MAUREEN *slops the porridge out and hands it to* MAG, *speaking as she does so.*

MAUREEN: You're oul and you're stupid and you don't know what you're talking about. Now shut up and eat your oul porridge.

MAUREEN *goes back to wash the pan in the sink.* MAG *glances at the porridge, then turns back to her.*

MAG: Me mug of tea you forgot!

MAUREEN *clutches the edges of the sink and lowers her head, exasperated, then quietly, with visible self-control, fills the kettle to make her mother's tea. Pause.* MAG *speaks while slowly eating.*

MAG: Did you meet anybody on your travels, Maureen? (*No response.*) Ah no, not on a day like today. (*Pause.*) Although you don't say hello to people is your trouble, Maureen. (*Pause.*) Although some people it would be better not to say hello to. The fella up and murdered the poor oul woman in Dublin and he didn't even know her. The news that story was on, did you hear of it? (*Pause.*) Strangled, and didn't even know her. That's a fella it would be better not to talk to. That's a fella it would be better to avoid outright.

MAUREEN *brings* MAG *her tea, then sits at the table.*

MAUREEN: Sure, that sounds exactly the type of fella I would *like* to meet, and then bring him home to meet you, if he likes murdering oul women.

MAG: That's not a nice thing to say, Maureen.

MAUREEN: Is it not, now?

MAG (*pause*): Sure why would he be coming all this way out from Dublin? He'd just be going out of his way.

MAUREEN: For the pleasure of me company he'd come. Killing you, it'd just be a bonus for him.

MAG: Killing *you* I bet he first would be.

MAUREEN: I could live with that so long as I was sure he'd be clobbering you soon after. If he clobbered you with a big axe or something and took your oul head off and spat in your neck, I wouldn't mind at all, going first. Oh no, I'd enjoy it, I would. No more oul Complan to get, and no more oul porridge to get, and no more . . .

MAG (*interrupting, holding her tea out*): No sugar in this, Maureen, you forgot, go and get me some.

MAUREEN *stares at her a moment, then takes the tea, brings it to the sink and pours it away, goes back to* MAG, *grabs her half-eaten porridge, returns to the kitchen, scrapes it out into the bin, leaves the bowl in the sink and exits into the hallway, giving* MAG *a dirty look on the way and closing the door behind her.* MAG *stares grumpily out into space. Blackout.*

SCENE TWO

MAG *is sitting at the table, staring at her reflection in a hand-mirror. She pats her hair a couple of times. The TV is on, showing an old episode of* The Sullivans. *There is a knock at the front door, which startles her slightly.*

MAG: Who . . . ? Maureen. Oh-h. The door, Maureen.

MAG *gets up and shuffles towards the kitchen window. There is another knock. She shuffles back to the door.*

Who's at the door?

RAY *(off):* It's Ray Dooley, Mrs. From over the way.

MAG: Dooley?

RAY: Ray Dooley, aye. You know me.

MAG: Are you one of the Dooleys so?

RAY: I am. I'm Ray.

MAG: Oh-h.

RAY *(pause. Irritated):* Well, will you let me in or am I going to talk to the door?

12

MAG: She's feeding the chickens. *(Pause.)* Have you gone?

RAY *(angrily)*: Open the oul door, Mrs! Haven't I walked a mile out of me way just to get here?

MAG: Have you?

RAY: I have. 'Have you?' she says.

MAG *unlatches the door with some difficulty and* RAY DOOLEY, *a lad of about twenty, enters.*

RAY: Thank you! An hour I thought you'd be keeping me waiting.

MAG: Oh, it's you, so it is.

RAY: Of course it's me. Who else?

MAG: You're the Dooley with the uncle.

RAY: It's only a million times you've seen me the past twenty year. Aye, I'm the Dooley with the uncle, and it's me uncle the message is.

RAY *stops and watches the TV a moment.*

MAG: Maureen's at the chickens.

RAY: You've said Maureen's at the chickens. What's on the telly?

MAG: I was waiting for the news.

RAY: You'll have a long wait.

MAG: I was combing me hair.

RAY: I think it's *The Sullivans*.

MAG: I don't know what it is.

13

RAY: You do get a good reception.

MAG: A middling reception.

RAY: Everything's Australian nowadays.

MAG: I don't know if it is or it isn't.

MAG *sits in the rocking-chair.*

At the chickens, Maureen is.

RAY: That's three times now you've told me Maureen's at the chickens. Are you going for the world's record in saying 'Maureen's at the chickens'?

MAG *(pause. Confused)*: She's feeding them.

RAY *stares at her a moment, then sighs and looks out through the kitchen window.*

RAY: Well, I'm not wading through all that skitter just to tell her. I've done enough wading. Coming up that oul hill.

MAG: It's a big oul hill.

RAY: It *is* a big oul hill.

MAG: Steep.

RAY: Steep is right and if not steep then muddy.

MAG: Muddy and rocky.

RAY: Muddy and rocky is right. Uh-huh. How do ye two manage up it every day?

MAG: We do drive.

RAY: Of course. *(Pause.)* That's what I want to do is drive. I'll have to be getting driving lessons. And a car. *(Pause.)* Not a good one, like. A second-hand one, y'know?

MAG: A used one.

RAY: A used one, aye.

MAG: Off somebody.

RAY: Oul Father Welsh—Walsh—has a car he's selling, but I'd look a poof buying a car off a priest.

MAG: I don't like Father Walsh—Welsh—at all.

RAY: He punched Mairtin Hanlon in the head once, and for no reason.

MAG: God love us!

RAY: Aye. Although, now, that was out of character for Father Welsh. Father Welsh seldom uses violence, same as most young priests. It's usually only the older priests go punching you in the head. I don't know why. I suppose it's the way they were brought up.

MAG: There was a priest in the news Wednesday had a babby with a Yank!

RAY: That's no news at all. That's everyday. It'd be hard to find a priest who hasn't had a babby with a Yank. If he'd punched that babby in the head, that'd be news. Aye. Anyways. Aye. What was I saying? Oh aye, so if I give you the message, Mrs, you'll be passing it on to Maureen, so you will, or will I be writing it down for you?

MAG: I'll be passing it on.

RAY: Good-oh. Me brother Pato said to invite yous to our uncle's going-away do. The Riordans' hall out in Carraroe.

MAG: Is your brother back so?

RAY: He is.

MAG: Back from England?

RAY: Back from England, aye. England's where he was, so that's where he would be back from. Our Yankee uncle's going home to Boston after his holiday and taking those two ugly duckling daughters back with him and that Dolores whatyoucall, Healey or Hooley, so there'll be a little to-do in the Riordans' as a goodbye or a *big* to-do knowing them show-off bastards and free food anyways, so me brother says ye're welcome to come or Maureen anyways, he knows you don't like getting out much. Isn't it you has the bad hip?

MAG: No.

RAY: Oh. Who is it has the bad hip so?

MAG: I don't know. I do have the urine infection.

RAY: Maybe that's what I was thinking of. And thanks for telling me.

MAG: Me urine.

RAY: I know, your urine.

MAG: And me bad back. And me burned hand.

RAY: Aye, aye, aye. Anyways, you'll be passing the message on to that one.

MAG: Eh?

RAY: You'll be remembering the message to pass it on to that one?

MAG: Aye.

RAY: Say it back to me so.

MAG: Say it back to you?

RAY: Aye.

MAG (*long pause*): About me hip . . . ?

RAY (*angrily*): I should've fecking written it down in the first fecking place, I fecking knew! And save all this fecking time!

RAY grabs a pen and a piece of paper, sits at the table and writes the message out.

Talking with a loon!

MAG (*pause*): Do me a mug of tea while you're here, Pato. Em, Ray.

RAY: *Ray* my fecking name is! Pato's me fecking brother!

MAG: I do forget.

RAY: It's like talking to a . . . talking to a . . .

MAG: Brick wall.

RAY: Brick wall is right.

MAG (*pause*): Or some soup do me.

RAY finishes writing and gets up.

17

RAY: There. Forget about soup. The message is there. Point that one in the direction of it when she returns from beyond. The Riordans' hall out in Carraroe. Seven o'clock tomorrow night. Free food. Okay?

MAG: All right now, Ray. Are you still in the choir nowadays, Ray?

RAY: I am *not* in the choir nowadays. Isn't it ten years since I was in the choir?

MAG: Doesn't time be flying?

RAY: Not since I took an interest in girls have I been in the choir because you do get no girls in choirs, only fat girls and what use are they? No. I go to discos, me.

MAG: Good enough for yourself.

RAY: What am I doing standing around here conversing with you? I have left me message and now I am off.

MAG: Goodbye to you, Ray.

RAY: Goodbye to you, Mrs.

MAG: And pull the door.

RAY: I was going to pull the door anyways . . .

RAY pulls the front door shut behind him as he exits.

(Off.) I don't need your advice!

As RAY's footsteps fade, MAG gets up, reads the message on the table, goes to the kitchen window and glances out, then finds a box of matches, comes back to the table, strikes a match, lights the message, goes to the range with it burning and drops it inside. Sound of footsteps approach-

ing the front door. MAG *shuffles back to her rocking-chair and sits in it just as* MAUREEN *enters.*

MAG *(nervously)*: Cold, Maureen?

MAUREEN: Of course cold.

MAG: Oh-h.

MAG stares at the TV as if engrossed. MAUREEN *sniffs the air a little, then sits at the table, staring at* MAG.

MAUREEN: What are you watching?

MAG: I don't know *what* I'm watching. Just waiting for the news I am.

MAUREEN: Oh aye. *(Pause.)* Nobody rang while I was out, I suppose? Ah no.

MAG: Ah no, Maureen. Nobody did ring.

MAUREEN: Ah no.

MAG: No. Who would be ringing?

MAUREEN: No, nobody I suppose. No. *(Pause.)* And nobody visited us either? Ah no.

MAG: Ah no, Maureen. Who would be visiting us?

MAUREEN: Nobody, I suppose. Ah no.

MAG glances at MAUREEN *a second, then back at the TV. Pause.* MAUREEN *gets up, ambles over to the TV, lazily switches it off with the toe of her shoe, ambles back to the kitchen, staring at* MAG *as she passes, turns on the kettle, and leans against the cupboards, looking back in* MAG's *direction.*

MAG (*nervously*): Em, apart from wee Ray Dooley who passed.

MAUREEN (*knowing*): Oh, did Ray Dooley pass, now?

MAG: He passed, aye, and said hello as he was passing.

MAUREEN: I thought just now you said there was no visitors.

MAG: There was no visitors, no, apart from Ray Dooley who passed.

MAUREEN: Oh, aye, aye, aye. Just to say hello he popped his head in.

MAG: Just to say hello and how is all. Aye. A nice wee lad he is.

MAUREEN: Aye. (*Pause.*) With no news?

MAG: With no news. Sure, what news would a gasur have?

MAUREEN: None at all, I suppose. Ah, no.

MAG: Ah, no. (*Pause.*) Thinking of getting a car I think he said he was.

MAUREEN: Oh aye?

MAG: A second-hand one.

MAUREEN: Uh-huh?

MAG: To drive, y'know?

MAUREEN: To drive, aye.

MAG: Off Father Welsh—Walsh—Welsh.

MAUREEN: Welsh.

MAG: Welsh.

MAUREEN *switches off the kettle, pours a sachet of Complan into a mug and fills it up with water.*

MAUREEN: I'll do you some of your Complan.

MAG: Have I not had me Complan already, Maureen? I have.

MAUREEN: Sure, another one won't hurt.

MAG *(wary)*: No, I suppose.

MAUREEN *tops the drink up with tap water to cool it, stirs it just twice to keep it lumpy, takes the spoon out, hands the drink to MAG, then leans back against the table to watch her drink it. MAG looks at it in distaste.*

MAG: A bit lumpy, Maureen.

MAUREEN: Never mind lumpy, Mam. The lumps will do you good. That's the best part of Complan is the lumps. Drink ahead.

MAG: A little spoon, do you have?

MAUREEN: No, I have no little spoon. There's no little spoons for liars in this house. No little spoons at all. Be drinking ahead.

MAG *takes the smallest of sickly sips.*

MAUREEN: The whole of it, now!

MAG: I do have a funny tummy, Maureen, and I do have no room.

MAUREEN: Drink ahead, I said! You had room enough to be spouting your lies about Ray Dooley had no message! Did I not meet him on the road beyond as he was going? The lies of you. The whole of that Complan you'll drink now, and suck the lumps down too, and whatever's left you haven't drank, it is over your head I will be emptying it, and you know well enough I mean it!

MAG *slowly drinks the rest of the sickly brew.*

MAUREEN: Arsing me around, eh? Interfering with my life again? Isn't it enough I've had to be on beck and call for you every day for the past twenty year? Is it one evening out you begrudge me?

MAG: Young girls should not be out gallivanting with fellas . . . !

MAUREEN: Young girls! I'm forty years old, for feck's sake! Finish it!

MAG *drinks again.*

MAUREEN: 'Young girls'! That's the best yet. And how did Annette or Margo ever get married if it wasn't first out gallivanting that they were?

MAG: I don't know.

MAUREEN: Drink!

MAG: I don't like it, Maureen.

MAUREEN: Would you like it better over your head?

MAG *drinks again.*

MAUREEN: I'll tell you, eh? 'Young girls out gallivanting.' I've heard it all now. What have I ever done but *kissed* two men the past forty year?

MAG: Two men is plenty!

MAUREEN: Finish!

MAG: I've finished!

MAG *holds out the mug.* MAUREEN *washes it.*

Two men is two men too much!

MAUREEN: To you, maybe. To you. Not to me.

MAG: Two men too much!

MAUREEN: Do you think I like being stuck up here with you? Eh? Like a dried up oul . . .

MAG: Whore!

MAUREEN *laughs.*

MAUREEN: 'Whore'? *(Pause.)* Do I not *wish*, now? Do I not wish? *(Pause.)* Sometimes I *dream* . . .

MAG: Of being a . . . ?

MAUREEN: Of anything! *(Pause. Quietly.)* Of anything. Other than this.

MAG: Well an odd dream that is!

MAUREEN: It's not at all. Not at all is it an odd dream. *(Pause.)* And if it is it's not the only odd dream I do have. Do you want to be hearing another one?

MAG: I don't.

MAUREEN: I have a dream sometimes there of you, dressed all nice and white, in your coffin there, and me all in black looking in on you, and a fella beside me there, comforting me, the smell of aftershave off him, his arm round me waist. And the fella asks me then if I'll be going for a drink with him at his place after.

MAG: And what do you say?

MAUREEN: I say 'Aye, what's stopping me now?'

MAG: You don't!

MAUREEN: I do!

MAG: At me funeral?

MAUREEN: At your bloody wake, sure! Is even sooner!

MAG: Well that's not a nice thing to be dreaming!

MAUREEN: I know it's not, sure, and it isn't a *dream*-dream at all. It's more of a day-dream. Y'know, something happy to be thinking of when I'm scraping the skitter out of them hens.

MAG: Not at all is that a nice dream. That's a mean dream.

MAUREEN: I don't know if it is or it isn't.

Pause. MAUREEN *sits at the table with a pack of Kimberley biscuits.*

I suppose now you'll never be dying. You'll be hanging on forever, just to spite me.

MAG: I *will* be hanging on forever!

MAUREEN: I know well you will!

MAG: Seventy you'll be at my wake, and then how many men'll there be round your waist with their aftershave?

MAUREEN: None at all, I suppose.

MAG: None at all is right!

MAUREEN: Oh aye. *(Pause.)* Do you want a Kimberley?

MAG (*pause*): Have we no shortbread fingers?

MAUREEN: No, you've ate all the shortbread fingers. Like a pig.

MAG: I'll have a Kimberley so, although I don't like Kimberleys. I don't know why you get Kimberleys at all. Kimberleys are horrible.

MAUREEN: Me world doesn't revolve around your taste in biscuits.

MAUREEN *gives* MAG *a biscuit.* MAG *eats.*

MAG (*pause*): You'll be going to this do tomorrow so?

MAUREEN: I will. (*Pause.*) It'll be good to see Pato again anyways. I didn't even know he was home.

MAG: But it's all them oul Yanks'll be there tomorrow.

MAUREEN: So?

MAG: You said you couldn't stand the Yanks yesterday. The crux of the matter yesterday you said it was.

MAUREEN: Well, I suppose now, Mother, I will have to be changing me mind, but, sure, isn't that a woman's prerogative?

MAG (*quietly*): It's only prerogatives when it suits you.

MAUREEN: Don't go using big words you don't understand, now, Mam.

MAG (*sneers. Pause*): This invitation was open to me too, if you'd like to know.

MAUREEN (*half-laughing*): Do you think you'll be coming?

MAG: I won't, I suppose.

MAUREEN: You suppose right enough. Lying the head off you, like the babby of a tinker.

MAG: I was only saying.

MAUREEN: Well, don't be saying. (*Pause.*) I think we might take a drive into Westport later, if it doesn't rain.

MAG (*brighter*): Will we take a drive?

MAUREEN: We could take a little drive for ourselves.

MAG: We could now. It's a while since we did take a nice drive. We could get some shortbread fingers.

MAUREEN: Later on, I'm saying.

MAG: Later on. Not just now.

MAUREEN: Not just now. Sure, you've only just had your Complan now.

MAG *gives her a dirty look. Pause.*

MAUREEN: Aye, Westport. Aye. And I think I might pick up a nice little dress for meself while I'm there. For the do to-morrow, y'know?

MAUREEN *looks across at* MAG, *who looks back at her, irritated. Blackout.*

SCENE THREE

Night. Set only just illuminated by the orange coals through the bars of the range. Radio has been left on low in the kitchen. Footsteps and voices of MAUREEN *and* PATO *are heard outside, both slightly drunk.*

PATO (*off. Singing*): 'The Cadillac stood by the house . . .'

MAUREEN (*off*): Shh, Pato . . .

PATO (*off. Singing quietly*): 'And the Yanks they were within.' (*Speaking.*) What was it that oul fella used to say, now?

MAUREEN (*off*): What oul fella, now?

MAUREEN *opens the door and the two of them enter, turning the lights on.* MAUREEN *is in a new black dress, cut quite short.* PATO *is a good-looking man of about the same age as her.*

PATO: The oul fella who used to chase oul whatyoucall. Oul Bugs Bunny.

MAUREEN: Would you like a cup of tea, Pato?

PATO: I would.

MAUREEN *switches the kettle on.*

MAUREEN: Except keep your voice down, now.

PATO (*quietly*): I will, I will. (*Pause.*) I can't remember *what* he used to say. The oul fella used to chase Bugs Bunny. It was something, now.

MAUREEN: Look at this. The radio left on too, the daft oul bitch.

PATO: Sure, what harm? No, leave it on, now. It'll cover up the sounds.

MAUREEN: What sounds?

PATO: The smooching sounds.

He gently pulls her to him and they kiss a long while, then stop and look at each other. The kettle has boiled. MAUREEN *gently breaks away, smiling, and starts making the tea.*

MAUREEN: Will you have a biscuit with your tea?

PATO: I will. What biscuits do you have, now?

MAUREEN: Em, only Kimberleys.

PATO: I'll leave it so, Maureen. I do hate Kimberleys. In fact I think Kimberleys are the most horrible biscuits in the world.

MAUREEN: The same as that, I hate Kimberleys. I only get them to torment me mother.

PATO: I can't see why the Kimberley people go making them at all. Coleman Connor ate a whole pack of Kimberleys one time and he was sick for a week. (*Pause.*) Or was it Mikados? It was some kind of horrible biscuits.

MAUREEN: Is it true Coleman cut the ears off Valene's dog and keeps them in his room in a bag?

PATO: He showed me them ears one day.

MAUREEN: That's awful spiteful, cutting the ears off a dog.

PATO: It *is* awful spiteful.

MAUREEN: It would be spiteful enough to cut the ears off anybody's dog, let alone your own brother's dog.

PATO: And it had seemed a nice dog.

MAUREEN: Aye. (*Pause.*) Aye.

Awkward pause. PATO *cuddles up behind her.*

PATO: You feel nice to be giving a squeeze to.

MAUREEN: Do I?

PATO: Very nice.

MAUREEN *continues making the tea as* PATO *holds her. A little embarrassed and awkward, he breaks away from her after a second and idles a few feet away.*

MAUREEN: Be sitting down for yourself, now, Pato.

PATO: I will. (*Sits at table.*) I do do what I'm told, I do.

MAUREEN: Oh-ho, do you now? That's the first time tonight I did notice. Them stray oul hands of yours.

PATO: Sure, I have no control over me hands. They have a mind of their own. (*Pause.*) Except I didn't notice you complaining overmuch anyways, me stray oul hands. Not too many complaints at all!

MAUREEN: I had complaints when they were straying over that Yank girl earlier on in the evening.

PATO: Well, I hadn't noticed you there at that time, Maureen. How was I to know the beauty queen of Leenane was still yet to arrive?

MAUREEN: 'The beauty queen of Leenane.' Get away with ya!

PATO: Is true!

MAUREEN: Why so have no more than two words passed between us the past twenty year?

PATO: Sure, it's took me all this time to get up the courage.

MAUREEN (*smiling*): Ah, bollocks to ya!

> PATO *smiles.* MAUREEN *brings the tea over and sits down.*

PATO: I don't know, Maureen. I don't know.

MAUREEN: Don't know what?

PATO: Why I never got around to really speaking to you or asking you out or the like. I don't know. Of course, hopping across to that bastarding oul place every couple of months couldn't've helped.

MAUREEN: England? Aye. Do you not like it there so?

PATO (*pause*): It's money. (*Pause.*) And it's Tuesday I'll be back there again.

MAUREEN: Tuesday? This Tuesday?

PATO: Aye. *(Pause.)* It was only to see the Yanks off I was over. To say hello and say goodbye. No time back at all.

MAUREEN: That's Ireland, anyways. There's always someone leaving.

PATO: It's always the way.

MAUREEN: Bad, too.

PATO: What can you do?

MAUREEN: Stay?

PATO *(pause)*: I do ask meself, if there was good work in Leenane, would I stay in Leenane? I mean, there never will be good work, but hypothetically, I'm saying. Or even bad work. Any work. And when I'm over there in London and working in rain and it's more or less cattle I am, and the young fellas cursing over cards and drunk and sick, and the oul digs over there, all pee-stained mattresses and nothing to do but watch the clock . . . when it's there I am, it's here I wish I was, of course. Who wouldn't? But when it's here I am . . . it isn't *there* I want to be, of course not. But I know it isn't here I want to be either.

MAUREEN: And why, Pato?

PATO: I can't put my finger on why. *(Pause.)* Of course it's beautiful here, a fool can see. The mountains and the green, and people speak. But when everybody knows everybody else's business . . . I don't know. *(Pause.)* You can't kick a cow in Leenane without some bastard holding a grudge twenty year.

MAUREEN: It's true enough.

PATO: It is. In England they don't care if you live or die, and it's funny but that isn't altogether a bad thing. Ah, sometimes it is . . . ah, I don't know.

MAUREEN (*pause*): Do you think you'll ever settle down in the one place so, Pato? When you get married, I suppose.

PATO (*half-laughing*): 'When I get married . . .'

MAUREEN: You will someday, I'll bet you, get married. Wouldn't you want to?

PATO: I can't say it's something I do worry me head over.

MAUREEN: Of course, the rake of women you have stashed all over, you wouldn't need to.

PATO (*smiling*): I have no rake of women.

MAUREEN: You have one or two, I bet.

PATO: I may have one or two. That I know to say hello to, now.

MAUREEN: Hello me . . . A-hole.

PATO: Is true. (*Pause.*) Sure, I'm no . . .

MAUREEN (*pause*): No what?

Pause. PATO *shrugs and shakes his head, somewhat sadly.*
Pause. The song 'The Spinning Wheel', sung by Delia
Murphy, has just started on the radio.

MAUREEN (*continued*): Me mother does love this oul song. Oul Delia Murphy.

PATO: This is a creepy oul song.

MAUREEN: It *is* a creepy oul song.

PATO: She does have a creepy oul voice. Always scared me this song did when I was a lad. She's like a ghoul singing. (*Pause.*) Does the grandmother die at the end, now, or is she just sleeping?

MAUREEN: Just sleeping, I think she is.

PATO: Aye . . .

MAUREEN (*pause*): While the two go hand in hand through the fields.

PATO: Aye.

MAUREEN: Be moonlight.

PATO (*nods*): They don't write songs like that any more. Thank Christ. (MAUREEN *laughs. Brighter.*) Wasn't it a grand night though, Maureen, now?

MAUREEN: It was.

PATO: Didn't we send them on their way well?

MAUREEN: We did, we did.

PATO: Not a dry eye.

MAUREEN: Indeed.

PATO: Eh?

MAUREEN: Indeed.

PATO: Aye. That we did. That we did.

MAUREEN (*pause*): So who *was* the Yankee girl you did have your hands all over?

PATO (*laughing*): Oh, will you stop it with your 'hands all over'?! Barely touched her, I did.

MAUREEN: Oh-ho!

PATO: A second cousin of me uncle, I think she is. Dolores somebody. Healey or Hooley. Healey. Boston, too, she lives.

MAUREEN: That was illegal so if it's your second cousin she is.

PATO: Illegal me arse, and it's not *my* second cousin she is anyway, and what's so illegal? Your second cousin's boobs aren't out of bounds, are they?

MAUREEN: They are!

PATO: I don't know about that. I'll have to consult with me lawyer on that one. I may get arrested the next time. And I have a defence anyways. She had dropped some Taytos on her blouse, there, I was just brushing them off for her.

MAUREEN: Taytos me arsehole, Pato Dooley!

PATO: Is true! (*Lustful pause. Nervously.*) Like this is all it was . . .

PATO *slowly reaches out and gently brushes at, then gradually fondles,* MAUREEN's *breasts. She caresses his hand as he's doing so, then slowly gets up and sits across his lap, fondling his head as he continues touching her.*

MAUREEN: She was prettier than me.

PATO: You're pretty.

MAUREEN: She was prettier.

PATO: I like you.

MAUREEN: You have blue eyes.

PATO: I do.

MAUREEN: Stay with me tonight.

PATO: I don't know, now, Maureen.

MAUREEN: Stay. Just tonight.

PATO *(pause)*: Is your mother asleep?

MAUREEN: I don't care if she is or she isn't. *(Pause.)* Go lower.

PATO *begins easing his hands down her front.*

MAUREEN: Go lower . . . Lower . . .

His hands reach her crotch. She tilts her head back slightly. The song on the radio ends. Blackout.

Scene Four

Morning. MAUREEN's *black dress is lying across the table.* MAG *enters from the hall carrying a potty of urine, which she pours out down the sink. She exits into the hall to put the potty away and returns a moment later, wiping her empty hands on the sides of her nightie. She spots the black dress and picks it up disdainfully.*

MAG: Forty pounds just for that skimpy dress? That dress is just skimpy. And laying it around then?

She tosses the dress into a far corner, returns to the kitchen and switches the kettle on, speaking loudly to wake MAUREEN.

I suppose I'll have to be getting me own Complan too, the hour you dragged yourself in whatever time it was with your oul dress. *(Quietly.)* That dress just looks silly. *(Loudly.)* Go the whole hog and wear no dress would be nearer the mark! *(Quietly.)* Snoring the head off you all night. Making an oul woman get her Complan, not to mention her porridge. Well, I won't be getting me own porridge, I'll tell you that now. I'd be afeard. You won't catch me getting me own porridge. Oh no. You won't be catching me out so easily.

PATO has just entered from the hall, dressed in trousers and pulling on a shirt.

PATO: Good morning there, now, Missus.

MAG is startled, staring at PATO dumbfounded.

MAG: Good morning there, now.

PATO: Is it porridge you're after?

MAG: It is.

PATO: I'll be getting your porridge for you, so, if you like.

MAG: Oh-h.

PATO: Go ahead and rest yourself.

MAG sits in the rocking chair, keeping her eyes on PATO all the while as he prepares her porridge.

PATO: It's many the time I did get me brother his porridge of a school morning, so I'm well accustomed. *(Pause.)* You couldn't make it to the oul Yanks' do yesterday so?

MAG: No.

PATO: Your bad hip it was, Maureen was saying.

MAG *(still shocked)*: Aye, me bad hip. *(Pause.)* Where's Maureen, now?

PATO: Em, having a lie-in a minute or two, she is. *(Pause.)* To tell you the truth, I was all for . . . I was all for creeping out before ever you got yourself up, but Maureen said 'Aren't we all adults, now? What harm?' I suppose we are, but . . . I don't know. It's still awkward, now, or something. D'you know what I mean? I don't know. (Pause.) The Yanks'll be touching down in Boston about now anyways. God willing anyways. Aye. (Pause.) A good oul send-off we gave them anyways, we did, to send them off. Aye. (Pause.) Not a dry eye. (Pause.) Aye. (Pause.) Was it a mug of Complan too you wanted?

MAG: It was.

PATO *fixes her Complan and brings it over.*

PATO: You like your Complan so.

MAG: I don't.

PATO: Do you not, now?

MAG: She makes me drink it when I don't like it and forces me.

PATO: But Complan's good for you anyways if you're old.

MAG: I suppose it's good for me.

PATO: It is. Isn't it chicken flavour?

MAG: I don't know what flavour.

PATO (*checking box*): Aye, it's chicken flavour. That's the best flavour.

PATO *returns to the porridge.*

MAG (*quietly*): With all oul lumps you do make it, never minding flavour. *And* no spoon.

PATO *gives* MAG *her porridge and sits at the table.*

PATO: There you go, now. *(Pause.)* Whatever happened to your hand there, Missus? Red raw, it is.

MAG: Me hand, is it?

PATO: Was it a scould you did get?

MAG: It *was* a scould.

PATO: You have to be careful with scoulds at your age.

MAG: Careful, is it? Uh-huh . . .

MAUREEN *enters from the hall, wearing only a bra and slip, and goes over to* PATO.

MAUREEN: Careful what? We was careful, weren't we, Pato?

MAUREEN *sits across* PATO's *lap.*

PATO *(embarrassed)*: Maureen, now . . .

MAUREEN: Careful enough, 'cos we don't need any babies coming, do we? We do have enough babies in this house to be going on with.

MAUREEN *kisses him at length.* MAG *watches in disgust.*

PATO: Maureen, now . . .

MAUREEN: Just thanking you for a wonderful night, I am, Pato. Well worth the wait it was. *Well* worth the wait.

PATO *(embarrassed)*: Good-oh.

MAG: Discussing me scoulded hand we was before you breezed in with no clothes!

MAUREEN: Ar, feck your scoulded hand. *(To* PATO.*)* You'll have to be putting that thing of yours in me again before too long is past, Pato. I do have a taste for it now, I do . . .

39

PATO: Maureen . . .

She kisses him, gets off, and stares at MAG *as she passes into the kitchen.*

MAUREEN: A mighty oul taste. Uh-huh.

PATO *gets up and idles around in embarrassment.*

PATO: Em, I'll have to be off now in a minute anyways. I do have packing to do I do, and whatyoucall . . .

MAG (*pointing at* MAUREEN. *Loudly*): *She*'s the one that scoulded me hand! I'll tell you that, now! Let alone sitting on stray men! Held it down on the range she did! Poured chip-pan fat o'er it! Aye, and told the doctor it was me!

MAUREEN (*pause. Nonplussed, to* PATO): Be having a mug of tea before you go, Pato, now.

PATO (*pause*): Maybe a quick one.

MAUREEN *pours out the tea.* MAG *looks back and forth between the two of them.*

MAG: Did you not hear what I said?!

MAUREEN: Do you think Pato listens to the smutterings of a senile oul hen?

MAG: Senile, is it? (*She holds up her left hand.*) Don't I have the evidence?

MAUREEN: Come over here a second, Pato. I want you to smell this sink for me.

MAG: Sinks have nothing to do with it!

MAUREEN: Come over here now, Pato.

PATO: Eh?

PATO *goes into the kitchen.*

MAUREEN: Smell that sink.

PATO *leans into the sink, sniffs it, then pulls his head away in disgust.*

MAG: Nothing to do with it, sinks have!

MAUREEN: Nothing to do with it, is it? Everything to do with it, *I* think it has. Serves as evidence to the character of me accuser, it does.

PATO: What is that, now? The drains?

MAUREEN: Not the drains at all. Not the drains at all. Doesn't she pour a potty of wee away down there every morning, though I tell her seven hundred times the lavvy to use, but oh no.

MAG: Me scoulded hand this conversation was, and not wee at all!

MAUREEN: And doesn't even rinse it either. Now is that hygienic? And she does have a urine infection too, is even less hygienic. I wash me praities in there. Here's your tea now, Pato.

PATO *takes his tea, sipping it squeamishly.*

MAG: Put some clothes on you, going around the house half-naked! Would be more in your line!

MAUREEN: I do like going around the house half-naked. It does turn me on, it does.

MAG: I suppose it does, aye.

41

MAUREEN: It does.

MAG: And reminds you of Difford Hall in England, too, I'll bet it does . . .

MAUREEN (angrily): Now you just shut your fecking . . .

MAG: None of your own clothes they let you wear in there either, did they?

MAUREEN: Shut your oul gob, I said . . . !

MAG: Only long oul gowns and buckle-down jackets . . .

MAUREEN approaches MAG, fists clenched. PATO catches her arm and steps between the two.

PATO: What's the matter with ye two at all, now . . . ?

MAG: Difford Hall! Difford Hall! Difford Hall . . . !

MAUREEN: Difford Hall, uh-huh. And I suppose . . .

MAG: Difford Hall! Difford Hall . . . !

MAUREEN: And I suppose that potty of wee was just a figment of me imagination?

MAG: Forget wee! Forget wee! D'you want to know what Difford Hall is, fella?

MAUREEN: Shut up, now!

MAG: It's a nut-house! An oul nut-house in England I did have to sign her out of and promise to keep her in me care. Would you want to be seeing the papers now?

MAG shuffles off to the hall.

As proof, like. Or to prove am I just a senile oul hen, like, or who's the loopy one? Heh! Pegging wee in me face, oh aye . . .

Quiet pause. MAUREEN *idles over to the table and sits.* PATO *pours his tea down the sink, rinses his mug and washes his hands.*

MAUREEN (*quietly*): It's true I was in a home there a while, now, after a bit of a breakdown I had. Years ago this is.

PATO: What harm a breakdown, sure? Lots of people do have breakdowns.

MAUREEN: A lot of doolally people, aye.

PATO: Not doolally people at all. A lot of well-educated people have breakdowns too. In fact, if you're well-educated it's even more likely. Poor Spike Milligan, isn't he forever having breakdowns? He hardly stops. I do have trouble with me nerves every now and then, too, I don't mind admitting. There's no shame at all in that. Only means you do think about things, and take them to heart.

MAUREEN: No shame in being put in a nut-house a month? Ah no.

PATO: No shame in thinking about things and worrying about things, I'm saying, and 'nut-house' is a silly word to be using, and you know that well enough, now, Maureen.

MAUREEN: I do.

PATO *goes over and sits across the table from her.*

MAUREEN: In England I was, this happened. Cleaning work. When I was twenty-five. Me first time over. Me only time over. Me sister had just got married, me other sister just about to. Over in Leeds I was, cleaning offices. Bogs. A whole group of us, only them were all English. 'Ya oul backward Paddy fecking . . . The fecking pig's-backside face on ya.' The first time out of Connemara this was I'd been. 'Get back to that backward fecking pigsty of yours or whatever hole it was you drug yourself out of.' Half of the swearing I didn't even understand. I had to have a black woman explain it to me. Trinidad she was from. They'd have a go at her too, but she'd just laugh. This big face she had, this big oul smile. And photos of Trinidad she'd show me, and 'What the hell have you left there for?' I'd say. 'To come to this place, cleaning shite?' And a calendar with a picture of Connemara on I showed her one day, and 'What the hell have you left there for?' she said back to me. 'To come to this place . . .' (*Pause.*) But she moved to London then, her husband was dying. And after that it all just got to me.

PATO (*pause*): That's all past and behind you now anyways, Maureen.

Pause. MAUREEN *looks at him a while.*

MAUREEN: Am I still a nut case you're saying, or you're wondering?

PATO: Not at all, now . . .

MAUREEN: Oh no . . . ?

MAUREEN *gets up and wanders back to the kitchen.*

PATO: Not at all. That's a long time in the past is all I'm saying. And nothing to be ashamed of. Put it behind you, you should.

MAUREEN: Put it behind me, aye, with that one hovering eyeing me every minute, like I'm some kind of . . . some kind of . . . (*Pause.*) And, no, I didn't scould her oul hand, no matter how doolally I ever was. Trying to cook chips on her own, she was. We'd argued, and I'd left her on her own an hour, and chips she up and decided she wanted. She must've tipped the pan over. God knows how, the eej. I just found her lying there. Only, because of Difford Hall, she thinks any accusation she throws at me I won't be any the wiser. I won't be able to tell the differ, what's true and what's not. Well, I *am* able to tell the differ. Well able, the smelly oul bitch.

PATO: You shouldn't let her get to you, Maureen.

MAUREEN: How can I help it, Pato? She's enough to drive anyone loopy, if they weren't loopy to begin with.

PATO (*smiling*): She is at that, I suppose.

MAUREEN (*smiling*): She is. It's surprised I am how sane I've turned out!

They both smile. Pause.

PATO: I *will* have to be off in a minute now, Maureen.

MAUREEN: Okay, Pato. Did you finish your tea, now?

PATO: I didn't. The talk of your mother's wee, it did put me off it.

MAUREEN: It would. It would anybody. Don't I have to live with it? (*Sadly.*) Don't I have to live with it? (*Looking straight at him.*) I suppose I do, now.

PATO (*pause*): Be putting on some clothes there, Maureen. You'll freeze with no fire down.

Pause. MAUREEN's *mood has become sombre again. She looks down at herself.*

MAUREEN (*quietly*): 'Be putting on some clothes'? Is it ugly you think I am now, so, 'Be putting on some clothes . . .'

PATO: No, Maureen, the cold, I'm saying. You can't go walking about . . . You'll freeze, sure.

MAUREEN: It wasn't ugly you thought I was last night, or maybe it was, now.

PATO: No, Maureen, now. What . . . ?

MAUREEN: A beauty queen you thought I was last night, or you said I was. When it's 'Cover yourself', now, 'You do sicken me' . . .

PATO (*approaching her*): Maureen, no, now, what are you saying that for . . . ?

MAUREEN: Maybe that was the reason so.

PATO (*stops*): The reason what?

MAUREEN: Be off with you so, if I sicken you.

PATO: You don't sicken me.

MAUREEN (*almost crying*): Be off with you, I said.

PATO (*approaching again*): Maureen . . .

MAG *enters, waving papers, stopping* PATO'*s approach.*

MAG: Eh? Here's the papers now, Difford Hall, if I'm such a senile oul hen. Eh? Who wants an oul read, now? Eh? Proof this is, let alone pegging sinks at me! (*Pause.*) Eh?

PATO: Maureen . . .

MAUREEN (*composed. Gently*): Be going now, Pato.

46

PATO *(pause)*: I'll write to you from England. *(Pause. Sternly.)* Look at me! *(Pause. Softly.)* I'll write to you from England.

PATO puts on his jacket, turns for a last look at MAUREEN, then exits, closing the door behind him. Footsteps away. Pause.

MAG: He won't write at all. *(Pause.)* And I did throw your oul dress in that dirty corner too!

Pause. MAUREEN looks at her a moment, sad, despairing but not angry.

MAUREEN: Why? Why? Why do you . . . ?

Pause. MAUREEN goes over to where her dress is lying, crouches down beside it and picks it up, holding it to her chest. She lingers there a moment, then gets up and passes her mother.

Just look at yourself.

MAUREEN exits into hall.

MAG: Just look at *your*self too, would be . . . would be . . . (MAUREEN *shuts the hall door behind her.*) . . . more in your line.

MAG is still holding up the papers rather dumbly. Pause. She lays the papers down, scratches herself, notices her uneaten porridge and sticks a finger in it. Quietly.

Me porridge is gone cold now. *(Loudly.)* Me porridge is gone cold now!

MAG stares out front, blankly. Blackout.

Interval.

Scene Five

Most of the stage is in darkness apart from a spotlight or some such on PATO *sitting at the table as if in a bedsit in England, reciting a letter he has written to* MAUREEN.

PATO: Dear Maureen, it is Pato Dooley and I'm writing from London, and I'm sorry it's taken so long to write to you but to be honest I didn't know whether you wanted me to one way or the other, so I have taken it upon myself to try and see. There are a lot of things I want to say but I am no letter-writer but I will try to say them if I can. Well, Maureen, there is no major news here, except a Wexford man on the site a day ago, a rake of bricks fell on him from the scaffold and forty stitches he did have in his head and was lucky to be alive at all, he was an old fella, or fifty-odd anyways, but apart from that there is no major news. I do go out for a pint of a Saturday or a Friday but I don't know nobody and don't speak to anyone. There is no one to speak to. The gangerman does pop his head in sometimes. I don't know if I've spelt it right, 'gangerman', is it 'e-r' or is it 'a'? It is not a word we was taught in school. Well, Maureen, I am 'beating around the bush' as they say, because it is you

48

and me I do want to be talking about, if there is such a thing now as 'you and me', I don't know the state of play. What I thought I thought we were getting on royally, at the goodbye to the Yanks and the part after when we did talk and went to yours. And I *did* think you were a beauty queen and I *do* think, and it wasn't anything to do with that at all or with you at all, I think you thought it was. All it was, it has happened to me a couple of times before when I've had a drink taken and was nothing to do with did I want to. I would have been honoured to be the first one you chose, and flattered, and the thing that I'm saying, I was honoured then and I am still honoured, and just because it was not to be that night, does it mean it is not to be ever? I don't see why it should, and I don't see why you was so angry when you was so nice to me when it happened. I think you thought I looked at you differently when your breakdown business came up, when I didn't look at you differently at all, or the thing I said 'Put on your clothes, it's cold', when you seemed to think I did not want to be looking at you in your bra and slip there, when nothing could be further from the truth, because if truth be told I could have looked at you in your bra and slip until the cows came home. I could never get my fill of looking at you in your bra and slip, and some day, God-willing, I will be looking at you in your bra and slip again. Which leads me on to my other thing, unless you still haven't forgiven me, in which case we should just forget about it and part as friends, but if you *have* forgiven me it leads me on to my other thing which I was lying to you before when I said I had no news because I do have news. What the news is I have been in touch with me uncle in Boston and the incident with the Wexford man with the bricks was just the final straw. You'd be lucky to get

49

away with your life the building sites in England, let alone the bad money and the 'You oul Irish this-and-that', and I have been in touch with me uncle in Boston and a job he has offered me there, and I am going to take him up on it. Back in Leenane two weeks tomorrow I'll be, to collect up my stuff and I suppose a bit of a do they'll throw me, and the thing I want to say to you is do you want to come with me? Not straight away of course, I know, because you would have things to clear up, but after a month or two I'm saying, but maybe you haven't forgiven me at all and it's being a fool I'm being. Well, if you haven't forgiven me I suppose it'd be best if we just kept out of each other's way the few days I'm over and if I don't hear from you I will understand, but if you *have* forgiven me what's to keep you in Ireland? There's your sisters could take care of your mother and why should you have had the burden all these years, don't you deserve a life? And if they say no, isn't there the home in Oughterard isn't ideal but they do take good care of them, my mother before she passed, and don't they have bingo and what good to your mother does that big hill do? No good. *(Pause.)* Anyways, Maureen, I will leave it up to you. My address is up the top there and the number of the phone in the hall, only let it ring a good while if you want to ring and you'll need the codes, and it would be grand to hear from you. If I don't hear from you, I will understand. Take good care of yourself, Maureen. And that night we shared, even if nothing happened, it still makes me happy just to think about it, being close to you, and even if I never hear from you again I'll always have a happy memory of that night, and that's all I wanted to say to you. Do think about it. Yours sincerely, Pato Dooley.

Spotlight cuts out, but while the stage is in darkness
PATO *continues with a letter to his brother.*

Dear Raymond, how are you? I'm enclosing a bunch of letters I don't want different people snooping in on. Will you hand them out for me and don't be reading them, I know you won't be. The one to Mick Dowd you can wait till he comes out of hospital. Let me know how he is or have they arrested the lass who belted him. The one to poor Girleen you can give to her any time you see her, it is only to tell her to stop falling in love with priests. But the one to Maureen Folan I want you to go over there the day you get this and put it in her hand. This is important now, in her hand put it. Not much other news here. I'll fill you in on more of the America details nearer the time. Yes, it's a great thing. Good luck to you, Raymond, and P.S. Remember now, in Maureen's hand put it. Goodbye.

Scene Six

Afternoon. RAY *is standing near the lit range, watching TV, somewhat engrossed, tapping a sealed envelope against his knee now and then.* MAG *watches him and the letter from the rocking-chair. Long pause before* RAY *speaks.*

RAY: That Wayne's an oul bastard.

MAG: Is he?

RAY: He is. He never stops.

MAG: Oh-h.

RAY (*pause*): D'you see Patricia with the hair? Patricia's bad enough, but Wayne's a pure terror. (*Pause.*) I do like *Sons and Daughters*, I do.

MAG: Do ya?

RAY: Everybody's always killing each other and a lot of the girls do have swimsuits. That's the best kind of programme.

MAG: I'm just waiting for the news to come on.

RAY *(pause)*: You'll have a long wait.

The programme ends. RAY *stretches himself.*

That's that then.

MAG: Is the news not next? Ah no.

RAY: No. For God's sake, *A Country Fecking Practice*'s on next. Isn't it Thursday?

MAG: Turn it off, so, if the news isn't on. That's all I do be waiting for.

RAY *turns the TV off and idles around.*

RAY: Six o'clock the news isn't on 'til. *(He glances at his watch. Quietly, irritated.)* Feck, feck, feck, feck, feck, feck, feck, feck, feck. *(Pause.)* You said she'd be home be now, didn't you?

MAG: I did. *(Pause.)* Maybe she got talking to somebody, although she doesn't usually get talking to somebody. She does keep herself to herself.

RAY: I know well she does keep herself to herself. *(Pause.)* Loopy that woman is, if you ask me. Didn't she keep the tennis ball that came off me and Mairtin Hanlon's swingball set and landed in yere fields and wouldn't give it back no matter how much we begged and that was ten years ago and I still haven't forgotten it?

MAG: I do have no comment, as they say.

RAY: Still haven't forgotten it and I never will forget it!

MAG: But wasn't it that you and Mairtin were pegging yere tennis ball at our chickens and clobbered one of them dead is why your ball was in our fields . . . ?

RAY: It was swingball we were playing, Missus!

MAG: Oh-h.

RAY: Not clobbering at all. Swingball it was. And never again able to play swingball were we. For the rest of our youth, now. For what use is a swingball set without a ball?

MAG: No use.

RAY: No use is right! No use at all *(Pause.) Bitch!*

MAG *(pause):* Be off and give your letter to me so, Ray, now, and I'll make sure she gets it, and not have you waiting for a lass ruined your swingball set on you.

RAY *thinks about it, tempted, but grudgingly decides against it.*

RAY: I'm under strict instructions now, Missus.

MAG *(tuts):* Make me a mug of tea so.

RAY: I'm not making you a mug of tea. Under duress is all I'm here. I'm not skivvying about on top of it.

MAG *(pause):* Or another bit of turf on the fire put. I'm cold.

RAY: Did I not just say?

MAG: Ah g'wan, Ray. You're a good boy, God bless you.

Sighing, RAY *puts the letter—which* MAG *stares at throughout—on the table and uses the heavy black poker beside the range to pick some turf up and place it inside, stoking it afterwards.*

RAY: Neverminding swingball, I saw her there on the road the other week and I said hello to her and what did she do? She outright ignored me. Didn't even look up.

MAG: Didn't she?

RAY: And what I thought of saying, I thought of saying, 'Up your oul hole, Missus', but I didn't say it, I just thought of saying it, but thinking back on it I should've gone ahead and said it and skitter on the bitch!

MAG: It would've been good enough for her to say it, up and ignoring you on the road, because you're a good gasur, Ray, fixing me fire for me. Ah, she's been in a foul oul mood lately.

RAY: She does wear horrible clothes. And everyone agrees. *(Finished at the range, poker still in hand,* RAY *looks over the tea-towel on the back wall.)* 'May you be half an hour in Heaven afore the Devil knows you're dead.'

MAG: Aye.

RAY *(funny voice)*: 'May you be half an hour in Heaven afore the Devil knows you're dead.'

MAG *(embarrassed laugh)*: Aye.

RAY *idles around a little, wielding the poker.*

RAY: This is a great oul poker, this is.

MAG: Is it?

RAY: Good and heavy.

MAG: Heavy and long.

RAY: Good and heavy and long. A half a dozen coppers you could take out with this poker and barely notice and have not a scratch on it and then clobber them again just for the fun of seeing the blood running out of them. *(Pause.)* Will you sell it to me?

MAG: I will not. To go battering the polis?

RAY: A fiver.

MAG: We do need it for the fire, sure.

RAY tuts and puts the poker back beside the range.

RAY: Sure, that poker's just going to waste in this house.

RAY idles into the kitchen. Her eye on the letter, MAG slowly gets out of her chair.

Ah, I could get a dozen pokers in town just as good if I wanted, and at half the price.

Just as MAG starts her approach to the letter, RAY returns, not noticing her, idles past and picks the letter back up on his way. MAG grimaces slightly and sits back down. RAY opens the front door, glances out to see if MAUREEN is coming, then closes it again, sighing.

A whole afternoon I'm wasting here. (*Pause.*) When I could be at home watching telly.

RAY sits at the table.

MAG: You never know, it might be evening before she's ever home.

RAY (*angrily*): You said three o'clock it was sure to be when I first came in!

MAG: Aye, three o'clock it usually is, oh aye. (*Pause.*) Just sometimes it does be evening. On occasion, like. (*Pause.*) Sometimes it does be *late* evening. (*Pause.*) Sometimes it does be *night*. (*Pause.*) *Morning* it was one time before she . . .

RAY *(interrupting angrily)*: All right, all right! It's thumping you in a minute I'll be!

MAG *(pause)*: I'm only saying now.

RAY: Well, stop saying! *(Sighs. Long pause.)* This house does smell of pee, this house does.

MAG *(pause. Embarrassed)*: Em, cats do get in.

RAY: Do cats get in?

MAG: They do. *(Pause.)* They do go to the sink.

RAY *(pause)*: What do they go to the sink for?

MAG: To wee.

RAY: To wee? They go to the sink to wee? *(Piss-taking.)* Sure, that's mighty good of them. You do get a very consider-ate breed of cat up this way so.

MAG *(pause)*: I don't know what breed they are.

Pause. RAY *lets his head slump down onto the table with a bump, and slowly and rhythmically starts banging his fist down beside it.*

RAY *(droning)*: I don't want to be here, I don't want to be here, I don't want to be here, I don't want to be here . . .

RAY *lifts his head back up, stares at the letter, then starts slowly turning it around, end over end, sorely tempted.*

MAG *(pause)*: Do me a mug of tea, Ray. *(Pause.)* Or a mug of Complan do me, even. *(Pause.)* And give it a good stir to get rid of the oul lumps.

RAY: If it was getting rid of oul lumps I was to be, it wouldn't be with Complan I'd be starting. It would be much closer to home, boy. Oh aye, much closer. A big lump sitting in an oul fecking rocking-chair it would be. I'll tell you that!

MAG (*pause*): Or a Cup-a-Soup do me.

RAY *grits his teeth and begins breathing in and out through them, almost crying.*

RAY (*giving in sadly*): Pato, Pato, Pato. (*Pause.*) Ah what news could it be? (*Pause. Sternly.*) Were I to leave this letter here with you, Missus, it would be straight to that one you would be giving it, isn't that right?

MAG: It is. Oh, straight to Maureen I'd be giving it.

RAY (*pause*): And it isn't opening it you would be?

MAG: It is not. Sure, a letter is a private thing. If it isn't my name on it, what business would it be of mine?

RAY: And may God strike you dead if you do open it?

MAG: And may God strike me dead if I do open it, only He'll have no need to strike me dead because I won't be opening it.

RAY (*pause*): I'll leave it so.

RAY *stands, places the letter up against a salt-cellar, thinks about it again for a moment, looks* MAG *over a second, looks back at the letter again, thinks once more, then waves a hand in a gesture of tired resignation, deciding to leave it.*

I'll be seeing you then, Missus.

MAG: Be seeing you, Pato. *Ray*, I mean.

RAY *grimaces at her again and exits through the front door, but leaves it slightly ajar, as he is still waiting outside.* MAG *places her hands on the sides of the rocking-chair, about to drag herself up, then warily remembers she hasn't heard* RAY's *footsteps away. She lets her hands rest back in her lap and sits back serenely. Pause. The front door bursts open and* RAY *sticks his head around it to look at her. She smiles at him innocently.*

RAY: Good-oh.

RAY *exits again, closing the door behind him fully this time.* MAG *listens to his footsteps fading away, then gets up, picks up the envelope and opens it, goes back to the range and lifts off the lid so that the flames are visible, and stands there reading the letter. She drops the first short page into the flames as she finishes it, then starts reading the second. Slow fade-out.*

SCENE SEVEN

Night. MAG *is in her rocking-chair,* MAUREEN *at the table, reading. The radio is on low, tuned to a request show. The reception is quite poor, wavering and crackling with static. Pause before* MAG *speaks.*

MAG: A poor reception.

MAUREEN: Can I help it if it's a poor reception?

MAG *(pause)*: Crackly. *(Pause.)* We can hardly hear the tunes. *(Pause.)* We can hardly hear what are the dedications or from what part of the country.

MAUREEN: I can hear well enough.

MAG: Can ya?

MAUREEN *(pause)*: Maybe it's deaf it is you're going.

MAG: It's not deaf I'm going. Not nearly deaf.

MAUREEN: It's a home for deaf people I'll have to be putting you in soon. *(Pause.)* And it isn't cod in butter sauce you'll be getting in there. No. Not by a long chalk. Oul beans on toast or something is all you'll be getting in

60

there. If you're lucky. And then if you don't eat it, they'll give you a good kick, or maybe a punch.

MAG *(pause)*: I'd die before I'd let meself be put in a home.

MAUREEN: Hopefully, aye.

MAG *(pause)*: That was a nice bit of cod in butter sauce, Maureen.

MAUREEN: I suppose it was.

MAG: Tasty.

MAUREEN: All I do is boil it in the bag and snip it with a scissor. I hardly need your compliments.

MAG *(pause)*: Mean to me is all you ever are nowadays.

MAUREEN: If I am or if I'm not. *(Pause.)* Didn't I buy you a packet of wine gums last week if I'm so mean?

MAG *(pause)*: All because of Pato Dooley you're mean, I suppose. *(Pause.)* Him not inviting you to his oul going-away do tonight.

MAUREEN: Pato Dooley has his own life to lead.

MAG: Only after one thing that man was.

MAUREEN: Maybe he was, now. Or maybe it was me who was only after one thing. We do have equality nowadays. Not like in your day.

MAG: There was nothing wrong in my day.

MAUREEN: Allowed to go on top of a man nowadays, we are. All we have to do is ask. And nice it is on top of a man, too.

MAG: Is it nice now, Maureen?

MAUREEN (*bemused that* MAG *isn't offended*): It is.

MAG: It does sound nice. Ah, good enough for yourself, now.

MAUREEN, *still bemused, gets some shortbread fingers from the kitchen and eats a couple.*

MAG: And not worried about having been put in the family way, are you?

MAUREEN: I'm not. We was careful.

MAG: Was ye careful?

MAUREEN: Aye. We was nice and careful. We was *lovely* and careful, if you must know.

MAG: I'll bet ye was lovely and careful, aye. Oh aye. Lovely and careful, I'll bet ye were.

MAUREEN (*pause*): You haven't been sniffing the paraffin lamps again?

MAG (*pause*): It's always the paraffin lamp business you do throw at me.

MAUREEN: It's a funny oul mood you're in so.

MAG: Is it a funny oul mood? No. Just a normal mood, now.

MAUREEN: It's a funny one. (*Pause.*) Aye, a great oul time me and Pato did have. I can see now what all the fuss did be about, but ah, there has to be more to a man than just being good in bed. Things in common too you do have to have, y'know, like what books do you be reading, or what are your politics and the like, so I did have to tell him it was no-go, no matter how good in bed he was.

MAG: When was this you did tell him?

MAUREEN: A while ago it was I did tell him. Back . . .

MAG (interrupting): And I suppose he was upset at that.

MAUREEN: He *was* upset at that but I assured him it was for the best and he did seem to accept it then.

MAG: I'll bet he accepted it.

MAUREEN (pause): But that's why I thought it would be unfair of me to go over to his do and wish him goodbye. I thought it would be awkward for him.

MAG: It would be awkward for him, aye, I suppose. Oh aye. (Pause.) So all it was was ye didn't have enough things in common was all that parted ye?

MAUREEN: Is all it was. And parted on amicable terms, and with no grudges on either side. (Pause.) No. No grudges at all. I did get what I did want out of Pato Dooley that night, and that was good enough for him, and that was good enough for me.

MAG: Oh aye, now. I'm sure. It was good enough for the both of ye. Oh aye.

MAG smiles and nods.

MAUREEN (laughing): It's a crazy oul mood you're in for yourself tonight!

Pause.

Pleased that tonight it is Pato's leaving and won't be coming pawing me again is what it is, I bet.

MAG: Maybe that's what it is. I *am* glad Pato's leaving.

63

MAUREEN (*smiling*): An interfering oul biddy is all you are. (*Pause.*) Do you want a shortbread finger?

MAG: I *do* want a shortbread finger.

MAUREEN: Please.

MAG: Please.

MAUREEN *gives* MAG *a shortbread finger, after waving it phallically in the air a moment.*

MAUREEN: Remind me of something, shortbread fingers do.

MAG: I suppose they do, now.

MAUREEN: I suppose it's so long since you've seen what they remind me of, you do forget what they look like.

MAG: I suppose I do. And I suppose you're the expert.

MAUREEN: I am the expert.

MAG: Oh aye.

MAUREEN: I'm the king of the experts.

MAG: I suppose you are, now. Oh, I'm sure. I suppose you're the king of the experts.

MAUREEN (*pause. Suspicious*): Why wouldn't you be sure?

MAG: With your Pato Dooley and your throwing it all in me face like an oul peahen, eh? When.... (MAG *catches herself before revealing any more.*)

MAUREEN (*pause. Smiling*): When what?

MAG: Not another word on the subject am I saying. I do have no comment, as they say. This is a nice shortbread finger.

MAUREEN (*with an edge*): When what, now?

MAG (*getting scared*): When nothing, Maureen.

MAUREEN (*forcefully*): No, when what, now? (*Pause.*) Have you been speaking to somebody?

MAG: Who would I be speaking to, Maureen?

MAUREEN (*trying to work it out*): You've been speaking to somebody. You've . . .

MAG: Nobody have I been speaking to, Maureen. You know well I don't be speaking to anybody. And, sure, who would Pato be telling about that . . . ?

> MAG *suddenly realises what she's said.* MAUREEN *stares at her in dumb shock and hate, then walks to the kitchen, dazed, puts a chip-pan on the stove, turns it on high and pours a half-bottle of cooking oil into it, takes down the rubber gloves that are hanging on the back wall and puts them on.* MAG *puts her hands on the arms of the rocking-chair to drag herself up, but* MAUREEN *shoves a foot against her stomach and groin, ushering her back.* MAG *leans back into the chair, frightened, staring at* MAUREEN, *who sits at the table, waiting for the oil to boil. She speaks quietly, staring straight ahead.*

MAUREEN: How do you know?

MAG: Nothing do I know, Maureen.

MAUREEN: Uh-huh?

MAG (*pause*): Or was it Ray did mention something? Aye, I think it was Ray . . .

MAUREEN: Nothing to Ray would Pato've said about that subject.

MAG (*tearfully*): Just to stop you bragging like an oul peahen, was I saying, Maureen. Sure what does an oul woman like me know? Just guessing, I was.

MAUREEN: You know sure enough, and guessing me arse, and not on me face was it written. For the second time and for the last time I'll be asking, now. How do you know?

MAG: On your face it *was* written, Maureen. Sure that's the only way I knew. You still do have the look of a virgin about you you always have had. (*Without malice.*) You always will.

Pause. The oil has started boiling. MAUREEN *rises, turns the radio up, stares at* MAG *as she passes her, takes the pan off the boil and turns the gas off, and returns to* MAG *with it.*

MAG: (*Terrified.*) A letter he did send you I read!

MAUREEN *slowly and deliberately takes her mother's shrivelled hand, holds it down on the burning range, and starts slowly pouring some of the hot oil over it, as* MAG *screams in pain and terror.*

MAUREEN: Where is the letter?

MAG (*through screams*): I did burn it! I'm sorry, Maureen!

MAUREEN: What did the letter say?

MAG *is screaming so much that she can't answer.* MAU-REEN *stops pouring the oil and releases the hand, which*

MAG *clutches to herself, doubled-up, still screaming, crying and whimpering.*

MAUREEN: What did the letter say?

MAG: Said he did have too much to drink, it did! Is why, and not your fault at all.

MAUREEN: And what else did it say?

MAG: He won't be putting me into no home!

MAUREEN: What are you talking about, no home? What else did it say?!

MAG: I can't remember, now, Maureen. I *can't* . . . !

MAUREEN *grabs* MAG's *hand, holds it down again and repeats the torture.*

MAG: No . . . !

MAUREEN: What else did it say?! Eh?!

MAG *(through screams)*: Asked you to go to America with him, it did!

Stunned, MAUREEN *releases* MAG's *hand and stops pouring the oil.* MAG *clutches her hand to herself again, whimpering.*

MAUREEN: What?

MAG: But how could you go with him? You do still have me to look after.

MAUREEN *(in a happy daze)*: He asked me to go to America with him? Pato asked me to go to America with him?

MAG *(looking up at her)*: But what about me, Maureen?

67

A slight pause before MAUREEN, *in a single and almost lazy motion, throws the considerable remainder of the oil into* MAG's *midriff, some of it splashing up into her face.* MAG *doubles-up, screaming, falls to the floor, trying to pat the oil off her, and lies there convulsing, screaming and whimpering.* MAUREEN *steps out of her way to avoid her fall, still in a daze, barely noticing her.*

MAUREEN (*dreamily, to herself*): He asked me to go to America with him . . . ? (*Recovering herself.*) What time is it? Oh feck, he'll be leaving! I've got to see him. Oh God . . . What will I wear? Uh . . . Me black dress! Me little black dress! It'll be a remembrance to him . . .

MAUREEN *darts off through the hall.*

MAG (*quietly, sobbing*): Maureen . . . help me . . .

MAUREEN *returns a moment later, pulling her black dress on.*

MAUREEN (*to herself*): How do I look? Ah, I'll have to do. What time is it? Oh God . . .

MAG: Help me, Maureen . . .

MAUREEN (*brushing her hair*): Help you, is it? After what you've done? Help you, she says. No, I won't help you, and I'll tell you another thing. If you've made me miss Pato before he goes, then you'll *really* be for it, so you will, and no messing this time. Out of me fecking way, now . . .

MAUREEN *steps over* MAG, *who is still shaking on the floor, and exits through the front door. Pause.* MAG *is still crawling around slightly. The front door bangs open and* MAG *looks up at* MAUREEN *as she breezes back in.*

Me car keys I forgot . . .

MAUREEN *grabs her keys from the table, goes to the door, turns back to the table and switches the radio off.*

Electricity.

MAUREEN *exits again, slamming the door. Pause. Sound of her car starting and pulling off. Pause.*

MAG (*quietly*): But who'll look after me, so?

MAG, *still shaking, looks down at her scalded hand. Blackout.*

SCENE EIGHT

Same night. The only light in the room emanates from the orange coals through the grill of the range, just illuminating the dark shapes of MAG, *sitting in her rocking-chair, which rocks back and forth of its own volition, her body unmoving, and* MAUREEN, *still in her black dress, who idles very slowly around the room, poker in hand.*

MAUREEN: To Boston. To Boston I'll be going. Isn't that where them two were from, the Kennedys, or was that somewhere else, now? Robert Kennedy I did prefer over Jack Kennedy. He seemed to be nicer to women. Although I haven't read up on it. *(Pause.)* Boston. It does have a nice ring to it. Better than England it'll be, I'm sure. Although where wouldn't be better than England? No shite I'll be cleaning there, anyways, and no names called, and Pato'll be there to have a say-so anyways if there was to be names called, but I'm sure there won't be. The Yanks do love the Irish. *(Pause.)* Almost begged me, Pato did. Almost on his hands and knees, he was, near enough crying. At the station I caught him, not five minutes to spare, thanks to you. Thanks to your oul interfering. But too late to be interfering you are now. Oh aye. Be far too late, although you did give it a good go, I'll say that for you. Another five minutes and you'd have had it. Poor you. Poor selfish oul bitch, oul you. *(Pause.)* Kissed the face off me, he did, when he saw me there. Them blue eyes of his. Them muscles. Them arms wrapping me. 'Why did you not answer me letter?' And all for coming over and giving you a good kick he was when I told him, but 'Ah no,' I said, 'isn't she just a feeble-minded oul feck, not worth dirtying your boots on?' I was defending you there. *(Pause.)* 'You will come to Boston with me so, me love, when you get up the money.' 'I will, Pato. Be it married or be it living in sin, what do I care? What do I care if tongues'd be wagging? Tongues have wagged about me before, let them wag again. Let them never stop wagging, so long as I'm with you, Pato, what do I care about tongues? So long as it's you and me, and the warmth of us cuddled up, and the skins of us asleep, is all I ever really wanted anyway.' *(Pause.)* 'Except we do still have a problem, what to do with your oul mam, there,' he said. 'Would an oul folks home be too harsh?' 'It wouldn't be too harsh but it would be too expensive.' 'What about your sisters so?' 'Me sisters wouldn't have the bitch. Not even a half-day at Christmas to be with her can them two stand. They clear forgot her birthday this year as well as that.' 'How do you stick her without going off your rocker?' they do say to me. Behind her back, like. *(Pause.)* 'I'll leave it up to yourself so,' Pato says. He was on the train be this time, we was kissing out the window, like they do in films. 'I'll leave it up to yourself so, whatever you decide. If it takes a month, let it take a month. And if it's finally you decide you can't bear to be parted from her and have to stay behind, well, I can't say I would like it, but I'd understand. But if even a year it has to take for you to decide, it is a year I will be waiting, and won't be minding the wait.' 'It won't be a year it is you'll be waiting, Pato', I called out then, the train was pulling away. 'It won't be a year nor yet nearly a year. It won't be a week!'

The rocking-chair has stopped its motions. MAG *starts to slowly lean forward at the waist until she finally topples over and falls heavily to the floor, dead. A red chunk of skull hangs from a string of skin at the side of her head.* MAUREEN *looks down at her, somewhat bored, taps her on the side with the toe of her shoe, then steps onto her back and stands there in thoughtful contemplation.*

'Twas over the stile she did trip. Aye. And down the hill she did fall. Aye. *(Pause.)* Aye.

Pause. Blackout.

SCENE NINE

A rainy afternoon. Front door opens and MAUREEN *enters in funeral attire, takes her jacket off and idles around quietly, her mind elsewhere. She lights a fire in the range, turns the radio on low and sits down in the rocking-chair. After a moment she half-laughs, takes down the boxes of Complan and porridge from the kitchen shelf, goes back to the range and empties the contents of both on the fire. She exits into the hall and returns a moment later with an old suitcase which she lays on the table, brushing off a thick layer of dust. She opens it, considers for a second what she needs to pack, then returns to the hall. There is a knock at the door.* MAUREEN *returns, thinks a moment, takes the suitcase off the table and places it to one side, fixes her hair a little, then answers the door.*

MAUREEN: Oh hello there, Ray.

RAY (*off*): Hello there, Missus . . .

MAUREEN: Come in ahead for yourself.

RAY: I did see you coming ahead up the road.

RAY *enters, closing the door.* MAUREEN *idles to the kitchen and makes herself some tea.*

I didn't think so early you would be back. Did you not want to go on to the reception or the whatyoucall they're having at Rory's so?

MAUREEN: No. I do have better things to do with me time.

RAY: Aye, aye. Have your sisters gone on to it?

MAUREEN: They have, aye.

RAY: Of course. Coming back here after, will they be?

MAUREEN: Going straight home, I think they said they'd be.

RAY: Oh aye. Sure, it's a long oul drive for them. Or fairly long. *(Pause.)* It did all go off okay, then?

MAUREEN: It did.

RAY: Despite the rain.

MAUREEN: Despite the rain.

RAY: A poor oul day for a funeral.

MAUREEN: It was. When it could've been last month we buried her, and she could've got the last of the sun, if it wasn't for the hundred bastarding inquests, proved nothing.

RAY: You'll be glad that's all over and done with now, anyways.

MAUREEN: Very glad.

RAY: I suppose they do only have their jobs to do. *(Pause.)* Although no fan am I of the bastarding polis. Me two wee toes they went and broke on me for no reason, me arse-hole drunk and disorderly.

MAUREEN: The polis broke your toes, did they?

RAY: They did.

MAUREEN: Oh. Tom Hanlon said what it was you kicked a door in just your socks.

RAY: Did he now? And I suppose you believe a policeman's word over mine. Oh aye. Isn't that how the Birmingham Six went down?

MAUREEN: Sure, you can't equate your toes with the Bir-mingham Six, now, Ray.

RAY: It's the selfsame differ. (*Pause.*) What was I saying, now?

MAUREEN: Some bull.

RAY: Some bull, is it? No. Asking about your mam's funeral, I was.

MAUREEN: That's what I'm saying.

RAY (*pause*): Was there a big turn-out at it?

MAUREEN: Me sisters and one of their husbands and nobody else but Maryjohnny Rafferty and oul Father Walsh— Welsh—saying the thing.

RAY: Father Welsh punched Mairtin Hanlon in the head once, and for no reason. (*Pause.*) Are you not watching telly for yourself, no?

MAUREEN: I'm not. It's only Australian oul shite they do ever show on that thing.

RAY *(slightly bemused)*: Sure, that's why I do like it. Who wants to see Ireland on telly?

MAUREEN: *I* do.

RAY: All you have to do is look out your window to see Ireland. And it's soon bored you'd be. 'There goes a calf.' *(Pause.)* I be bored anyway. I be continually bored. *(Pause.)* London I'm thinking of going to. Aye. Thinking of it, anyways. To work, y'know. One of these days. Or else Manchester. They have a lot more drugs in Manchester. Supposedly, anyways.

MAUREEN: Don't be getting messed up in drugs, now, Ray, for yourself. Drugs are terrible dangerous.

RAY: Terrible dangerous, are they? Drugs, now?

MAUREEN: You know full well they are.

RAY: Maybe they are, maybe they are. But there are plenty of other things just as dangerous, would kill you just as easy. Maybe even easier.

MAUREEN *(wary)*: Things like what, now?

RAY *(pause. Shrugging)*: This bastarding town for one.

MAUREEN *(pause. Sadly)*: Is true enough.

RAY: Just that it takes seventy years. Well, it won't take me seventy years. I'll tell you that. No way, boy. *(Pause.)* How old was your mother, now, when she passed?

MAUREEN: Seventy, aye. Bang on.

RAY: She had a good innings, anyway. *(Pause.)* Or an innings, anyway. *(Sniffs the air.)* What's this you've been burning?

MAUREEN: Porridge and Complan I've been burning.

RAY: For why?

MAUREEN: Because I don't eat porridge or Complan. The re-
mainders of me mother's, they were. I was having a
good clear-out.

RAY: Only a waste that was.

MAUREEN: Do I need your say-so so?

RAY: I'd've been glad to take them off your hands, I'm saying.

MAUREEN (*quietly*): I don't need your say-so.

RAY: The porridge, anyway. I do like a bit of porridge. I'd've
left the Complan. I don't drink Complan. Never had no
call to.

MAUREEN: There's some Kimberleys left in the packet I was
about to burn too, you can have, if it's such a big thing.

RAY: I *will* have them Kimberleys. I do love Kimberleys.

MAUREEN: I bet you do.

RAY *eats a couple of Kimberleys.*

RAY: Are they a bit stale, now? (*Chews.*) It does be hard to tell
with Kimberleys. (*Pause.*) I think Kimberleys are me
favourite biscuits out of any biscuits. Them or Jaffa
Cakes. (*Pause.*) Or Wagon Wheels. (*Pause.*) Or would
you classify Wagon Wheels as biscuits at all now. Aren't
they more of a kind of a bar . . . ?

MAUREEN (*interrupting*): I've things to do now, Ray. Was it
some reason you had to come over or was it just to dis-
cuss Wagon Wheels?

RAY: Oh aye, now. No, I did have a letter from Pato the other day and he did ask me to come up.

MAUREEN *sits in the rocking-chair and listens with keen interest.*

MAUREEN: He did? What did he have to say?

RAY: He said sorry to hear about your mother and all, and his condolences he sent.

MAUREEN: Aye, aye, aye, and anything else, now?

RAY: That was the main gist of it, the message he said to pass onto you.

MAUREEN: It had no times or details, now?

RAY: Times or details? No . . .

MAUREEN: I suppose . . .

RAY: Eh?

MAUREEN: Eh?

RAY: Eh? Oh, also he said he was sorry he didn't get to see you the night he left, there, he would've liked to've said goodbye. But if that was the way you wanted it, so be it. Although rude, too, I thought that was.

MAUREEN *(standing, confused)*: I did see him the night he left. At the station, there.

RAY: What station? Be taxicab Pato left. What are you thinking of?

MAUREEN *(sitting)*: I don't know now.

RAY: Be taxicab Pato left, and sad that he never got your goodbye, although why he wanted your goodbye I don't know. *(Pause.)* I'll tell you this, Maureen, not being harsh, but your house does smell an awful lot nicer now that your mother's dead. I'll say it does, now.

MAUREEN: Well, isn't that the best? With me thinking I did see him the night he left, there. The train that pulled away.

He looks at her as if she's mad.

RAY: Aye, aye. *(Mumbled, sarcastic.)* Have a rest for yourself. *(Pause.)* Oh, do you know a lass called, em . . . Dolores Hooley, or Healey, now? She was over with the Yanks when they was over.

MAUREEN: I know the name, aye.

RAY: She was at me uncle's do they had there, dancing with me brother early on. You remember?

MAUREEN: Dancing with him, was it? Throwing herself at him would be nearer the mark. Like a cheap oul whore.

RAY: I don't know about that, now.

MAUREEN: Like a cheap oul whore. And where did it get her?

RAY: She did seem nice enough to me, there, now. Big brown eyes she had. And I do like brown eyes, me, I do. Oh aye. Like the lass used to be on *Bosco*. Or I *think* the lass used to be on *Bosco* had brown eyes. We had a black and white telly at that time. *(Pause.)* What was I talking about, now?

MAUREEN: Something about this Dolores Hooley or whoever she fecking is.

RAY: Oh aye. Herself and Pato did get engaged a week ago, now, he wrote and told me.

MAUREEN (*shocked*): Engaged to do what?

RAY: Engaged to get married. What do you usually get engaged for? 'Engaged to do what?' Engaged to eat a bun!

MAUREEN *is dumbstruck.*

RAY: A bit young for him, I think, but good luck to him. A whirlwind oul whatyoucall. July next year, they're thinking of having it, but I'll have to write and tell him to move it either forward or back, else it'll coincide with the European Championships. I wonder if they'll have the European Championships on telly over there at all? Probably not, now, the Yankee bastards. They don't care about football at all. Ah well. (*Pause.*) It won't be much of a change for her anyways, from Hooley to Dooley. Only one letter. The 'h'. That'll be a good thing. (*Pause.*) Unless it's Healey that she is. I can't remember. (*Pause.*) If it's Healey, it'll be three letters. The 'h', the 'e' and the 'a'. (*Pause.*) Would you want me to be passing any message on, now, when I'm writing, Missus? I'm writing tomorrow.

MAUREEN: I get . . . I do get confused. Dolores Hooley . . . ?

RAY (*pause. Irritated*): Would you want me to be passing on any message, now, I'm saying?

MAUREEN (*pause*): Dolores Hooley . . . ?

RAY (*sighing*): Fecking . . . The loons you do get in this house! Only repeating!

MAUREEN: Who's a loon?

RAY: Who's a loon, she says!

RAY *scoffs and turns away, looking out the window.* MAU-
REEN *quietly picks up the poker from beside the range
and, holding it low at her side, slowly approaches him
from behind.*

MAUREEN *(angrily)*: Who's a loon?!

RAY *suddenly sees something hidden behind a couple of
boxes on the inner window ledge.*

RAY *(angrily)*: Well, isn't that fecking just the fecking best
yet . . . !

RAY *picks up a faded tennis ball with a string sticking out
of it from the ledge and spins around to confront* MAU-
REEN *with it, so angry that he doesn't even notice the
poker.* MAUREEN *stops in her tracks.*

Sitting on that fecking shelf all these fecking years
you've had it, and what good did it do ya?! A tenner that
swingball set did cost me poor ma and da and in 1979
that was, when a tenner was a lot of money. The best
fecking present I did ever get and only two oul months'
play out of it I got before you went and confiscated it on
me. What right did you have? What right at all? No
right. And just left it sitting there then to fade to fecking
skitter. I wouldn't've minded if you'd got some use out
of it, if you'd taken the string out and played pat-ball or
something agin a wall, but no. Just out of pure spite is
the only reason you kept it, and right under me fecking
nose. And then you go wondering who's a fecking loon?
Who's a fecking loon, she says. I'll tell you who's a fecking loon, lady. *You're* a fecking loon!

MAUREEN *lets the poker fall to the floor with a clatter and sits in the rocking-chair, dazed.*

MAUREEN: I don't know why I did keep your swingball on you, Raymond. I can't remember at all, now. I think me head was in a funny oul way in them days.

RAY: 'In them days,' she says, as she pegs a good poker on the floor and talks about trains.

RAY picks the poker up and puts it in its place.

That's a good poker, that is. Don't be banging it against anything hard like that, now.

MAUREEN: I won't.

RAY: That's an awful good poker. *(Pause.)* To show there's no hard feelings over me swingball, will you sell me that poker, Missus? A fiver I'll give you.

MAUREEN: Ah, I don't want to be selling me poker now, Ray.

RAY: G'wan. Six!

MAUREEN: No. It does have sentimental value to me.

RAY: I don't forgive you, so!

MAUREEN: Ah, don't be like that, now, Ray . . .

RAY: No, I don't forgive you at all . . .

RAY goes to the front door and opens it.

MAUREEN: Ray! Are you writing to your brother, so?

RAY *(sighing)*: I am. Why?

MAUREEN: Will you be passing a message on from me?

RAY (*sighs*): Messages, messages, messages, messages! What's the message, so? And make it a short one.

MAUREEN: Just say . . .

MAUREEN *thinks about it a while.*

RAY: This week, if you can!

MAUREEN: Just say . . . Just say, 'The beauty queen of Leenane says hello.' That's all.

RAY: 'The beauty queen of Leenane says hello.'

MAUREEN: Aye. No!

RAY *sighs again.*

MAUREEN: *Goodbye*. Goodbye. 'The beauty queen of Leenane says *goodbye*.'

RAY: 'The beauty queen of Leenane says goodbye.' Whatever the feck that means, I'll pass it on. 'The beauty queen of Leenane says goodbye', although after this fecking swingball business, I don't see why the feck I should. Goodbye to you so, Missus . . .

MAUREEN: Will you turn the radio up a biteen too, before you go, there, Pato, now? *Ray*, I mean . . .

RAY (*exasperated*): Feck . . .

RAY *turns the radio up.*

The exact fecking image of your mother you are, sitting there pegging orders and forgetting me name! Goodbye!

MAUREEN: And pull the door after you . . .

RAY (*shouting angrily*): I was going to pull the fecking door after me!!

RAY *slams the door behind him as he exits. Pause.* MAU-REEN *starts rocking slightly in the chair, listening to the song by The Chieftains on the radio. The announcer's quiet, soothing voice is then heard.*

ANNOUNCER: A lovely tune from The Chieftains there. This next one, now, goes out from Annette and Margo Folan to their mother Maggie, all the way out in the mountains of Leenane, a lovely part of the world there, on the occasion of her seventy-first birthday last month now. Well, we hope you had a happy one, Maggie, and we hope there'll be a good many more of them to come on top of it. I'm sure there will. This one's for you, now.

'The Spinning Wheel' by Delia Murphy is played. MAU-REEN *gently rocks in the chair until about the middle of the fourth verse, when she quietly gets up, picks up the dusty suitcase, caresses it slightly, moves slowly to the hall door and looks back at the empty rocking-chair a while. It is still rocking gently. Slight pause, then* MAU-REEN *exits into the hall, closing its door behind her as she goes. We listen to the song on the radio to the end, as the chair gradually stops rocking and the lights, very slowly, fade to black.*

A Skull in Connemara

A Skull in Connemara, a Druid Theatre Company/
Royal Court Theatre co-production, was first presented at the Town Hall Theatre, Galway, on June 3,
1997, and subsequently opened at the Royal Court
Theatre Downstairs on July 17, 1997. The cast was as
follows:

MICK DOWD	Mick Lally
MARY RAFFERTY	Anna Manahan
MAIRTIN HANLON	David Wilmot
TOM HANLON	Brian F. O'Byrne

Directed by Garry Hynes
Designed by Francis O'Connor
Lighting design by Ben Ormerod
Sound design by Bell Helicopter
Music by Paddy Cunneen

Characters

MICK DOWD, *fifties.*
MARYJOHNNY RAFFERTY, *seventies.*
MAIRTIN HANLON, *late teens/early twenties.*
THOMAS HANLON, *his brother, thirties.*

Setting: Rural Galway.

SCENE ONE

The fairly spartan main room of a cottage in rural Galway. Front door stage left, a table with two chairs and a cupboard towards the right, and a lit fireplace in the centre of the back wall with an armchair on each side of it. A crucifix hangs on the back wall and an array of old farm tools, sickles, scythes and picks, etc., hang just below it. At the start of the play, MICK DOWD, a man in his fifties whose cottage it is, is sitting in the left armchair as MARY RAFFERTY, a heavy-set, white-haired neighbour in her seventies, knocks and is let in through the front door.

MARY: Mick.

MICK: Maryjohnny.

MARY: Cold.

MICK: I suppose it's cold.

MARY: Cold, aye. It's turning.

MICK: Is it turning?

MARY: It's turning now, Mick. The summer is going.

MICK: It isn't going yet, or is it now?

MARY: The summer is going, Mick.

MICK: What month are we now?

MARY: Are we September?

MICK *(thinks)*: We are, d'you know?

MARY: The summer is going.

MICK: What summer we had.

MARY: What summer we had. We had no summer.

MICK: Sit down for yourself, there, Mary.

MARY *(sitting)*: Rain, rain, rain, rain, rain we had. And now the cold. And now the dark closing in. The leaves'll be turning in a couple of weeks, and that'll be the end of it.

MICK: I didn't even know it *was* September, and I'll admit it.

MARY: Did you not now, Mick? What month did you think it was?

MICK: August or something I thought it was.

MARY: August? *(Laughs.)* August is gone.

MICK: I know it is, now.

MARY: August went.

MICK: I know it did.

MARY: Last month August was.

MICK *(slightly irritated)*: I know it was now, Mary. You don't have to keep saying.

MARY (*pause*): Didn't the boys and girls go back to school, and stopped parading up and down the street like . . .

MICK: Ah sure they did. And don't I usually notice that one, and say to meself, 'The boys and girls have gone back to school. The summer is surely over now.'

MARY: Like a pack o' whores.

MICK (*pause*): Who's like a pack o' whores?

MARY: Them schoolies parading up and down.

MICK: I wouldn't say a pack o' whores, now.

MARY: Kissing.

MICK: What harm?

MARY: Cursing.

MICK: Mary, you're too old-fashioned, so you are. Who doesn't curse nowadays?

MARY: I don't.

MICK: 'You don't.'

MARY (*pause*): Eamonn Andrews didn't.

MICK: Well we can't all be as good as you or Eamonn Andrews. And I'll bet Eamonn Andrews would've cursed too were he to've fell, or sat on a nail.

MARY: He would not.

MICK: It's only on television you ever saw. When he got home he probably cursed a-plenty. He probably did nothing but curse.

MARY: Oh, a lie now . . .

MICK: When he got home now, I'm saying.

MARY: I'll tell you someone else who doesn't curse. *(Pointing to the crucifix.)* That man doesn't curse.

MICK: Well we can't all be as good as Our Lord. Let alone Eamonn Andrews. Now those youngsters are only out for a bit of fun during their holidays, and not meaning no harm to anybody.

MARY: No harm to anybody, is it, Mick? And the three I caught weeing in the churchyard and when I told them I'd tell Father Cafferty, what did they call me? A fat oul biddy!

MICK: I know they did, Mary, and they shouldn't've . . .

MARY: I know well they shouldn't've!

MICK: That was twenty-seven years ago for God's sake, Mary.

MARY: Twenty-seven years ago or not!

MICK: You should let bygones be bygones.

MARY: Bygones, is it? No, I will not let bygones be bygones. I'll tell you when I'll let bygones be bygones. When I see them burned in hell I'll let bygones be bygones, and not before!

MICK: Hell is too harsh a price just for weeing. Sure they were only five, God bless them.

MARY: On consecrated ground, Mick.

MICK: On consecrated ground or not. They may have been bursting. And what's consecrated ground anyways but any old ground with a dab of holy water pegged on it?

MARY: Well, you would be the man, Mick Dowd, I'd expect would argue that, the filthy occupation you take on every autumntime . . .

MICK (*interrupting*): There's no need for that.

MARY: Is there no need for that, now?

MICK *gets up, pours out two glasses of poteen, gives one to* MARY *and sits down with the other.*

MICK: Doesn't the County pay for the job to be done if it's such a filthy occupation? Doesn't the priest half the time stand over me and chat to me and bring me cups of tea? Eh?

MARY (*pause*): I suppose he does. (*Sips her poteen.*) Not that I'd give a bent ha'penny for that young skitter.

MICK: What young skitter?

MARY: Father Welsh, Walsh, Welsh.

MICK: Nothing the matter with Father Welsh.

MARY: Nothing the matter at all, except I don't too much like going to confession with a gasur aged two!

MICK: What the hell sins do you have to confess to him every week anyways?

MARY: What sins do *you* confess would be more in your line.

MICK (*playfully*): What would it be, now? It wouldn't be impure thoughts? Ah no. It must be 'Thou shalt not steal' so.

MARY: How, 'Thou shalt not steal'?

MICK: Oh, cadging off the Yanks a pound a throw the maps the Tourist Board asked you to give them for free. Telling them your Liam's place was where *The Quiet Man* was filmed, when wasn't it a hundred miles away in Ma'am Cross or somewhere?

MARY: A hundred miles is it? Ma'am Cross has moved so, because eight miles it was the last time I looked.

MICK: John Wayne photos, two pound a pop. Maureen O'Hara drank out of this mug—a fiver. Boy, I'll tell you, anh? Them eejit Yanks.

MARY: If the eejit Yanks want to contribute a couple of bob to an oul lady's retirement, I'll not be standing in their way, sure.

MICK: So if it's not cadging off them thicks you confess it must be playing the ten books the bingo, so.

MARY *(smiling)*: I don't play ten books the bingo.

MICK: Oh, the County could round up a hundred witnesses would tell you the differ, 'cos twenty year it's been going on now.

MARY: Maybe now and then I do forget how many books I've picked up . . .

MICK: Forget, is it?

MARY *(slightly hurt)*: It's forget, Mick. I do mean to pick up the four, and then two books get stuck together, and before I know where I am I'm sitting down and how many books do I have . . .

MICK: Mary Rafferty, you have played ten books in that church hall for every week since de Valera was twelve, and it's ten books if they're lucky, because doesn't it rise to fifteen when the Christmas jackpot draws on, and isn't it twenty-two books at once your Guinness World's Record is, and wouldn't it be higher still if it wasn't eighteen times you won that night and you thought they might begin to get suspicious?

MARY *stares at him angrily.*

MARY: Well on the subject of confession, now, Mick Dowd, how long is it since *you've* seen the priest? Seven and a half years, is it, Mick?

MICK: Eh?

MARY: Seven and a half . . .

MICK *(angrily)*: That's enough of that, now, Mary.

MARY: Wasn't it your Oona used to drag you there of a week . . . ?

MICK *(angrily, standing)*: That's enough of that now, I said! Or else be off with you!

He idles a little, pouring himself another drink.

MARY: He calls too slow anyways.

MICK: Who calls too slow?

MARY: That skitter at St Patrick's the bingo.

MICK: Oh, calls the bingo.

MARY: Walsh, Welsh. *(Pause.)* You need ten books to make it worthwhile, else you'd be hanging about, so. It isn't to win I have ten books.

MICK: It's the game of it.

MARY: It's the game of it, Mick, is right.

MICK: Nobody begrudges you anyways.

MARY: Because I'm oul.

MICK: Nobody begrudges you still.

A knock at the front door, which pushes open imme-diately. MAIRTIN *enters in a Manchester United away shirt, blowing bubbles now and then.*

MAIRTIN: How is all?

MARY: How are you, Mairtin?

MICK: How are you, Mairtin? And close the door.

MAIRTIN: I'll close the door (*Does so.*) or was it a barn with a wide open door you were born in, me mam says. She says, was it a barn with a wide open door you were born in, Mary beag, and I say 'You're the get would know, Mam.'

MARY *tuts.*

MAIRTIN: No, I say, you're the woman would know, Mam. I do. That's what I say, like. Because if anybody was to know where I was born, wouldn't it be her? (*Pause.*) The Regional Hospital I was born. In Galway.

MICK: We know where the Regional Hospital is.

MAIRTIN: Aye. (*To* MARY.) Wasn't it you was in there with your hip?

MARY: No.

MAIRTIN: It must've been somebody else so. Aye. Who was it? Somebody who fell down and was fat.

MICK: What is it you've come over about, Mairtin?

MAIRTIN: Father Welsh or Walsh sent me over. It was choir and I was disruptive. Is that poteen, Mick? You wouldn't spare a drop?

MICK: No I wouldn't.

MAIRTIN: Ah g'wan . . .

MARY: Why was you being disruptive in choir, Mairtin? You used to be a good little singer, God bless you.

MAIRTIN: Ah, a pack of oul shite they sing now.

MARY *tuts at his language.*

MAIRTIN: A pack of not very good songs they sing now, I mean. All wailing, and about fishes, and bears.

MICK: About fishes and bears, is it?

MAIRTIN: It is. That's what *I* said, like. They said no, the youngsters like these ones. What's the song they had us singing tonight? Something about if I was a bear I'd be happy enough, but I'm even more glad I'm human. Ah, a pile of oul wank it is. It's only really the Christmas carols I do like.

MICK: And in September you don't get too much call for them.

MAIRTIN: Is right, you don't. But I think they should have them all year, instead of the skitter they do, because they do make you very Christmassy, like.

MARY: How is Mam and Dad, Mairtin, I haven't seen them a few days?

MAIRTIN: Oh, grand indeed, now. Or anyway me mam's grand and me dad's as grand as a bastard of a get like him can be . . .

MARY: Mairtin. Your own father now.

MAIRTIN: My own father is right. And if he took his belt off to you for no reason at all eight times a week, it wouldn't be so quick you'd be saying 'Your own father now'. I'll tell you that.

MICK: And you don't do anything to deserve it, I suppose? Ah no.

MAIRTIN: Not a thing.

MICK: Not a thing, oh aye. Not even the guards' tyres got slashed outside the disco in Carraroe, your pal Ray Dooley got nabbed for, someone else ran away.

MAIRTIN: Wasn't me now, Mick.

MICK: Oh no. Of course.

MAIRTIN: I had a bad leg anyways, and what were the guards doing in the disco that time of night anyway is what I'd like to know.

MICK: Routing out the yobbos who started the bottle fight that the two wee girls got taken the night to hospital from.

MAIRTIN: Well you'd think they'd have something better to do with their time.

MICK: Uh-huh. What was Welsh's message, Mairtin?

MAIRTIN: And maybe them two girls deserved a bottling anyways. You don't know the full facts.

MARY: Why would poor girls deserve a bottling, sure?

MAIRTIN: Every why. Maybe the piss out of a fella's trainers they took, when all he did was ask them for a danceen, and polite. And then called their bastard brother over to come the hard. Stitches aren't good enough for them sorts of bitches, and well they know. As ugly as them two started out, sure stitches'd be nothing but an improvement, oh aye. (*Pause.*) But as I say, I wasn't there, now, I had a bad leg.

MICK: Are you going to make me ask me question again, Mairtin?

MAIRTIN: What question?

MICK: What was Welsh's fecking message, for Christ's sake?!

MAIRTIN (*pause*): Shouting is it, Mick? You're to make a start on this year's exhuming business this coming week. The graveyard shenanigans.

MARY *looks across at* MICK *with stern resentment.* MICK *avoids her gaze somewhat guiltily.*

MICK: This coming week? That's early. In the year, I mean. Although with them burying poor Mag Folan last month there I suppose has hurried things along a little.

MAIRTIN: I don't know if it's hurried things along a little and I don't care if it's hurried things along a little. I'm to help you anyways and twenty quid the week oul Walsh, oul Welsh is to be giving me.

MICK: You're to help me?

MAIRTIN: Oul Welsh said. Aye. Twenty quid the week. How much do you get the week, Mick?

MICK: I get enough the week, and what matter is it to you?

MAIRTIN: No matter at all, now. Only wondering, I was.

MICK: Well don't be wondering.

MAIRTIN: Sure, you're the experienced man, anyways. If it's a hundred or if it's more than a hundred, you deserve it, for you're the experienced man. (*Pause.*) Is it more than a hundred, Mick, now?

MICK: This ladeen.

MAIRTIN: Sure I'm only asking, sure.

MICK: Well that's what you do best is ask eejit questions.

MAIRTIN: Oh, eejit questions, is it?

MICK: It is.

MAIRTIN: Ah . . . ah . . . hmm.

MARY: It's more than you, Mairtin, has questions that that man will not answer.

MICK: Oh, now you're starting with your oul woman bull.

MAIRTIN: What kind of questions, Mary beag?

MARY: Questions about where did he put our Padraig when he dug him up is the kind of question, and where did he put our Bridgit when he dug her up is the kind of question, and where did he put my poor ma and da when he dug them up is the biggest question!

MAIRTIN: Where *did* you put all Mary's relations, Mick then, now? The oul bones and the whatnot.

MARY: He won't let on.

MICK: Will I not let on?

MARY: Let on so.

MAIRTIN: Aye, let on so.

MICK: Oh, now you're chipping in.

MAIRTIN: I *am* chipping in. What did you do with them?

MICK: What did I do with them, is it?

MAIRTIN: It is. For the hundredth fecking time it is.

MICK: Oh, for the hundredth fecking time, is it? I'll tell you what I did with them. I hit them with a hammer until they were dust and I pegged them be the bucketload into the slurry.

MARY *is aghast.* MAIRTIN *bursts out laughing loudly.*

MAIRTIN *(laughing)*: Is that true, now?

MICK: Oh, maybe it's true now, and maybe it isn't at all.

MAIRTIN: You hit them with a hammer and you pegged them in the slurry? Can I do that, now, Mick?

MICK: No, you can't do that.

MAIRTIN: Ah, you don't hammer no corpses at all. Probably seal them up and put them somewhere is all you do. Put them in the lake or somewhere, when no beggar's about.

MICK: Maybe it's in the lake I put them, aye. This is the expert.

MARY *has been keeping* MICK *in a stern, fixed stare all the while.*

MARY: Mick Dowd!

MICK: Maryjohnny!

MARY: I am going to ask you one question! And I want the truth!

MICK: Ask away for yourself!

MARY: Is that right what you said that you hammer the bones to nothing and you throw them in the slurry?

MICK: What I do with the bones, both the priest and the guards have swore me to secrecy and bound by them I am . . .

MAIRTIN: Oh ho.

MARY (standing): Michael Dowd, if you do not answer, bound or not bound, I shall leave this devil-taken house and never darken its . . . !

MICK: Bound I am by the priest and the guards . . .

MARY: Michael Dowd, if you do not answer . . .

MICK: I neither hammer the bones nor throw them in the slurry, Mary. Sure what do you take me for?

MAIRTIN: I knew well, sure . . .

MARY: So what is it you do with them so, if it isn't hammer?

MICK (pause): I seal them in a bag and let them sink to the bottom of the lake and a string of prayers I say over them as I'm doing so.

MAIRTIN: I told you, now, it was the fecking lake, or the lake rather. Didn't I tell you now that that's what it was, that he sealed them in a bag and he pegged them in the lake?

MICK: I didn't say I pegged them. I said I gently *eased* them.

MAIRTIN: Oh aye, you eased them in there, like. And said a couple of prayers over them, aye.

MICK: And said a couple of prayers over them.

MAIRTIN: To make it official, like.

MARY: Is that the truth, Mick Dowd?

MICK: That's the truth, Mary beag.

MARY: I shall sit and finish that sup with you, so.

MICK: Good on you, Mary.

MARY *sits back down.* MICK *refills her glass.*

MAIRTIN (*eyeing the poteen*): After seven years, sure, it's only a poor straggle of two or three bones they are anyway, I'm sure, and nothing to hammer at all.

MICK: The expert on the matter now we're listening to.

MAIRTIN: It's nothing to do with expert. Pure oul common sense is all it has to do with.

MICK: Now you're explaining it to me.

MAIRTIN: There's been a cow in our field dead four or five years . . .

MICK: I know there has. And that's the best cow you have.

MAIRTIN: No, no, now. Not the best cow we have. It wasn't even our cow at all. Didn't it just wander into our fields one day and fall over dead?

MICK: Aye. The smell knocked it.

MAIRTIN: And isn't it now just the . . . 'The smell knocked it.' Feck you. The smell of this house? Eh? 'The smell knocked it'? I'll tell you, boy, eh? *(Pause.)* What was it I was saying, now? You've made me forget . . .

MICK: 'Isn't it now just the something . . .'

MAIRTIN: Isn't it now just the skull and a couple of bones left on it, the cow, and no hide nor hair other than that? So wouldn't the body of a person be even less than that, it being rotting in the ground?

MICK: You have a point there. Except the body of a person your family wouldn't have been picking at for yer dinners the last five years.

MAIRTIN: Picking at it for our dinners, is it? We do have a sight better dinners in our house than you do in this fecking house anyways! I'll tell you that now! Poteen breakfasts and poteen suppers is all I ever see consumed in this house!

MICK: True enough for yourself.

MAIRTIN: Eh? Insulting our mam's dinners, when all it was was explaining about the cow in our field and the bones was all I was doing. Explaining, so as to help you.

MICK: You're right there, now, Mairtin. I wasn't thinking.

MAIRTIN: Right? I know I'm right.

MICK: And if I insulted you or your mam or your mam's dinners by casting aspersions you pick the meat off cows five years dead and can't tell the differ, then I take it all back and I apologise.

MAIRTIN: *(confused)*: Eh? Uh-huh? Well, okay. Good.

MICK *pours himself another drink.*

MAIRTIN: And just to show there's no hard feelings, the tiniest of sips, now, let me take a taste of, Mick. This much, even.

MICK: That much, is it?

MAIRTIN: That's all. To show there's no hard feelings, now.

MICK: To show there's no hard feelings, aye.

He pours a small amount of poteen out onto his fingers and tosses it at MAIRTIN *as if it's holy water. It hits* MAIRTIN *in the eyes.*

Bless yourself, now, Mairtin.

MARY *laughs slightly.* MICK *sits back down.* MAIRTIN *rubs his eyes angrily.*

MAIRTIN: Got me in the eye, that did!

MICK: Sure that's where I was aiming. I'll bet it stung too.

MAIRTIN: It *did* sting too, you stinking fecker you. (MARY *tuts.*) Tut at me, you? Tut at him would be more in your line when he throws poteen in me eyes, near blinds me.

MARY: You'll know now not again to be disruptive in choir, Mairtin beag.

MAIRTIN: Choir?! What has fecking choir to do with anything?! He insults me mam's cooking, throws poteen in me eyes.

MICK: Sure it was only a drop, sure. Would I be wasting good poteen on your eyes?

MAIRTIN (*to* MARY): Has it gone red, Gran?

MARY: A bit red, Mairtin . . .

MICK: 'Gone red.' Jeez, you always was a wussy oul pussy, Mairtin, and nothing but a wussy oul pussy.

MAIRTIN: A wussy oul pussy, is it?

MICK: It is.

MAIRTIN: Well maybe I am at that, and maybe I know something that you don't know too.

MICK: What do you know? Skitter you know, Mairtin beag.

MAIRTIN: Maybe I know which corner of the cemetery it is we're to be digging this week.

MICK: What do I care which corner of the cemetery?

MAIRTIN: Oh, maybe you don't, now. Only that it's the south side, by the gable.

MICK *nods, somewhat disturbed.*

MICK: Are they all more than seven years down, then, at the gable. They are, I suppose.

MAIRTIN: They are. Seven years and more! *(To* MARY.*)* See? He doesn't like it when it starts to get closer to home. That's when he doesn't like it.

MARY: What do you mean, 'closer to home'?

MAIRTIN: Isn't it his missus buried down there by the gable? How closer to home can you get?

MARY: Is Oona buried at the gable, Mick, now?

MICK: She is.

MARY: Oh, God love you . . .

MAIRTIN: That'll be an interesting job anyways. It isn't many's the man gets paid for digging up the bones of his own dead wife.

MICK: Oona left those bones a long time ago, and that's the only thing that they are now, is bones.

MARY (*quietly*): You can't go digging up Oona, Mick. That's not right. Leave Oona to somebody else, now.

MICK: To who? To him? He'd probably crack her head in two, so he would.

MAIRTIN: Oh. Crack her head in two, is it?

MICK: It is.

MAIRTIN: I heard that's already been done.

MICK (*pause. Standing, advancing*): What did you hear?

MAIRTIN: Just a thing or two, now, and don't you be fecking advancing on me, because saying nothing I was, only some people say things and I pay no mind at all until some other people start shouting the odds and calling me names and pegging poteen in me eyes . . .

MICK: What names did I call you?

MARY (*pause. Quietly*): A wussy oul pussy . . .

MAIRTIN: A wussy oul pussy you called me. And if people start doing that then I'll have to be pegging something back at them, and it isn't a smatter of poteen it'll be, it'll be aspersions. And if the aspersions are true or not I don't know, and I don't care. I only threw them out because it was you who started the whole shebang in the first place.

MICK: What *are* the aspersions anyways?

MAIRTIN: Just general ones.

MICK: The only aspersions that could be cast are the ones I've already admitted to, and the ones I've already served me time over. That I had had a drink taken, and a good drink, and that she had no seat-belt on her, and that was the end of it. No other aspersions could there be.

MAIRTIN: Well, sure, that was the aspersion I was saying anyways, the drink-driving aspersion. What aspersion did you think I was saying?

MICK (*pause*): That was the aspersion you was saying?

MAIRTIN: Aye. (*Pause.*) What was . . .

MICK: Well even that aspersion is seven years past, yet straight to me face you go casting your fecking . . .

MAIRTIN: Well isn't that better than the most of them round here? Will smile at you 'til you're a mile away before they start talking behind your back. One thing about me, anyways. I'm honest.

MICK (*to* MARY): Do people be talking behind my back?

MARY: They do not. He's a wee get with nothing but cheek.

MAIRTIN: A wee get is it? And they don't be talking behind his back? Uh-huh. It must be some other fella who drove his wife into a wall, so, they must be talking about. I must be mistaken. I often am.

MICK (*quietly*): Leave this house, Mairtin Hanlon.

MAIRTIN: I *will* leave this house, the welcome I got here, after coming all this way with the message from oul Welsh, Walsh, Welsh. Not only no welcome but a spray of poteen that almost took me eyes out as a thank you, not to mention the names called, and the insulted mam's dinners. Uh-huh. *(Exits. Reenters.)* Um . . . will they have a spade at the church I can use, Mick, for I have no spade?

MARY: Your father has a rake of spades, sure.

MAIRTIN: My father has no rake of spades. He has a rake of rakes. He has no spade. The only spade he has are the handles of two spades, and nothing but the handles, which you couldn't call a spade at all. Rakes he has a stack of, and I don't know why, because there is no call for them. There is always more call for a spade than a rake. In my opinion.

MICK: They'll have a spade at the church.

MAIRTIN: Will they have a spade at the church? Except they'll need two spades. One for the both of us . . .

MICK: They'll have two spades.

MAIRTIN: Are you positive, now? I don't want to be walking all that way . . .

MICK: Mairtin, will you ever feck off home for yourself?!

MAIRTIN: Feck off home, is it? I'll feck off home, all right. I don't have to be asked twice.

MICK: No, fecking five times you have to be asked!

MAIRTIN (*exiting*): Uh-huh, I don't have to be asked twice.

MARY (*pause*): The tongue on that one.

Pause. They drink their poteen a while, staring into the fire.

MICK: Is it true, Mary?

MARY: Is what true, Mick?

MICK: The talking behind my back.

MARY: There is no talking behind your back. He's a wee eejit, or if not an eejit then a blackguard, and we both know the truth of that.

MICK: Aye.

MARY: Sure the time he put the werewolf comic in with Mrs Dunphy, and hadn't they almost nailed the lid on her before we noticed?

MICK: Aye.

MARY: If that had gone ahead, just think. (*Pause.*) The boy's a wee blackguard and nothing else, and even though he's me own grandson I'll admit it, he's a rotten blackguard with nothing but cheek, so don't you even be thinking about it.

MICK: Aye. (*Pause.*) Aye, I suppose you're right.

MARY: I *am* right, sure.

MICK: Aye.

MARY: Right? There's no question, right.

MICK: There's not, I suppose. No. (*Pause.*) No. (*Pause.*) And there's been no other aspersions cast with my name on them, other than those . . .

MARY: There's been no other aspersions, Mick. (*Pause.*) None at all, sure. (*Pause.*) Sure we all know the type of man you are, Mick Dowd.

MICK *looks across at her.*

MICK: Aye . . . Is right.

MARY *smiles at him slightly. They both stare at the fire again. Curtain.*

Scene Two

A rocky cemetery at night, lit somewhat eerily by a few lamps dotted about. Two graves with gravestones atop a slight incline in the centre. At the start of the scene, the grave on the right is in the process of being dug up by MICK, standing down inside it to waist height, shoveling the dirt out. MAIRTIN lays his shovel down, sits against the right-hand gravestone behind him, and lights a cigarette.

MAIRTIN: I'm taking a cigarette break.

MICK: A break from what, sure? You've done no work.

MAIRTIN: I've done my biteen.

MICK: A bit of shite you've done.

MAIRTIN: I have a blister too, and I didn't even mention it.

MICK: You've mentioned it now.

MAIRTIN: For fear I'd be accused of complaining. *(Pause. Looking at the next-door grave.)* When will we be starting on your missus's patch anyways? Going around in circles to avoid it we seem to be.

MICK: We go in order. We don't skip two ahead.

MAIRTIN: Skip? That's all we've been doing is skipping, if you're asking my opinion. (*Pause.*) I'll make a start on your missus's grave.

MICK: Will you, now?

MAIRTIN: I may.

> MAIRTIN *takes his shovel and idles past* MICK *to Oona's grave.* MICK *stops work and looks at him threateningly.* MAIRTIN *taps the soil with his foot, then raises his shovel as if about to start digging.*

MICK: One grain of that soil you touch, Mairtin Hanlon, it is *in* that grave you will be, not on it.

> MAIRTIN *smiles, lays his shovel aside, and leans against the gravestone behind him.*

MAIRTIN: Is it murder you're threatening now, Mick, and in earshot of your missus too?

MICK: It isn't murder, because self-defence it would be, as protection from your wittering on like a fecking oul hen. I would be doing the community a service.

MAIRTIN: The community a service? I heard you already did the community a service.

MICK: What service?

MAIRTIN: The community service you did, when they let you out of jail early.

MICK: Now you're starting again.

> MICK *returns to his digging.*

MAIRTIN: I'm just saying, like.

MICK: Now you're trying to come the clever.

MAIRTIN: Well, as I say to Sheila Fahey, it isn't too hard I have to try to come the clever, because I *am* clever.

MICK: Clever, is it? And is it ten times you've failed the Leaving Certificate now, or is it eleven times?

MAIRTIN: It's one time.

MICK: Oh, is it one time, now?

MAIRTIN: The other time it coincided with me wrongful expulsion.

MICK: Your wrongful expulsion? Uh-huh. The cat you cooked alive in biology?

MAIRTIN: It wasn't me at all, now, Mick, and they knew full well it wasn't me, and didn't they have to reinstate me on the spot when Blind Billy Pender came out and confessed, with not a word of apology from them.

MICK: Poor backward Blind Billy Pender, aye, whom you didn't influence in his confession at all.

MAIRTIN: And it was a hamster anyways, if you would like to get your facts right.

MICK: I don't need help from the likes of you to get me facts right.

MAIRTIN: Oh aye.

MICK: I'll tell you that anyways.

MAIRTIN (*pause*): Let's get a start on your missus's grave, Mick.

MICK (*pause*): We'll get a start when we've finished this one. And when the guard arrives.

MAIRTIN: When the guard arrives? Oh. Is there a law, so, you can't dig up your wife unless you have the polis there?

MICK: Something of the like. Or, anyways, the guard had a word, said I'd best make sure he was there before we made a start. To save tongues wagging anyways.

MAIRTIN: What would tongues be wagging for?

MICK: I don't know. Just for the sake of it.

Sound of MICK'S *shovel hitting the rotten wood at the bottom of the grave.*

MAIRTIN: Are you through to him?

MICK: Pass me the sack down.

MAIRTIN *jumps up from where he is and looks down into the grave. Sound of* MICK *jimmying rotten wood apart with his shovel. He picks the bits of wood up and throws them out of the grave.* MAIRTIN *moves around a little to get a better view of the corpse.*

MAIRTIN: Ay yi yi, look at that one. Who is he? (*Glances behind.*) Daniel Faragher. Never heard of him.

MICK: I knew him to say hello to.

MAIRTIN: Would you recognise him?

MICK *looks at* MAIRTIN *as if he's stupid.*

MAIRTIN: Not from his bare skull, no, of course. Although he still has a lock of hair there, now. He looks like a big dolly.

MICK: A what?

MAIRTIN: A big dolly. Like girls do play with.

MICK: The girls won't be playing with this dolly.

MAIRTIN: I know that, sure. I'm only saying. How old would he be, then?

MICK: He would be . . .

MAIRTIN: No, let me guess, now.

MICK: Guess ahead.

MAIRTIN: A pound if I guess right.

MICK: And a pound to me if you guess wrong.

MAIRTIN: Okay. (*Glances at headstone and calculates.*) He was, I'd say . . . about sixty-seven now.

MICK: Wrong. *Seventy*-seven he was. You owe me a pound.

MAIRTIN *looks back at the headstone again, recalculates on his fingers, and realises his mistake.*

MAIRTIN: Ah feck.

MICK: And pass me the sack, for the fiftieth time.

MAIRTIN *goes off mumbling behind the headstones.*

MAIRTIN: I'll pass you the fecking sack . . .

. . . *and returns with a large, dirty black cloth sack half-full of the bones and skulls of two corpses.* MAIRTIN *passes it to* MICK.

Pass your skull to me, Mick. Just to compare, now.

MICK *tosses* MAIRTIN *the skull with the lock of hair on it, then starts placing the bones from the grave into the sack, keeping a quiet eye on* MAIRTIN *all the while as he idles around with the skulls, placing them against his chest as if they're breasts at one point, kissing them together at another.*

MAIRTIN: Sure skulls are great oul things. It's hard to believe you have one of these on the inside of your head.

MICK: It's hard to believe *you* have one of them anyways, and the brain to go with it.

MAIRTIN: I have no brain, is it? I have a brain too, and a big brain.

MICK: Kissing skulls together. Like an oul schoolgirl.

MAIRTIN *(pause)*: When do oul schoolgirls kiss skulls together, sure?

MICK *(pause)*: I'm just saying, like.

MAIRTIN: Oul schoolgirls can't get ahold of skulls at all.

He pokes a finger in the skulls' eye sockets.

You can stick your fingers right in their eyes.

MICK *(pause. Confused)*: Oul schoolgirls' eyes, now?

MAIRTIN: Skulls' eyes, now! Why would you be sticking your fingers in schoolgirls' eyes?

MICK: I don't know, now.

MAIRTIN *hands the skulls back to* MICK *who places them in the sack, then quietly crouches down and looks into the grave.*

115

MAIRTIN: Hey, Mick!

MICK: What?

MAIRTIN: Where does your thing go?

MICK: Eh?

MAIRTIN: Where does your thing go? When you die, I mean. None of them have had their things at all. And I've looked.

MICK: I know well you've looked. And the women's too! I think that's why you came on this job, to have a good look. You don't see many living ones.

MAIRTIN: I see my share.

MICK: Of willies, now, Mairtin?

MAIRTIN: Of the other, and you know well!

MICK: Do you really not know where they go? Have you never been told?

MAIRTIN: No.

MICK: They don't tell you in religious studies?

MAIRTIN: No. I do skip a lot of religious studies. It's just a lot of stuff about Jesus.

MICK: That's the reason you don't know, so. Isn't it illegal in the Catholic faith to bury a body the willy still attached? Isn't it a sin in the eyes of the Lord?

MAIRTIN (incredulous): No . . .

MICK: Don't they snip them off in the coffin and sell them to tinkers as dog food.

MAIRTIN (*horrified*): They do not!

MICK: And during the famine, didn't the tinkers stop feeding them to their dogs at all and start sampling the merchandise themselves?

MAIRTIN: They did not, now, Mick . . .

MICK: You would see them riding along with them, munching ahead.

MAIRTIN: No . . .

MICK: That's the trouble with young people today, is they don't know the first thing about Irish history.

MICK smiles to himself. MAIRTIN, *sickened, sees this and begins to doubt.*

MAIRTIN: That isn't true.

MICK: As true as I'm standing here.

MAIRTIN: I'll go up and ask oul Walsh, Welsh, at the church so. He'd be the man to know.

MICK: Go ahead, so.

MAIRTIN: Eh?

MICK: Go on ahead and ask for yourself.

MAIRTIN: I *will* go on ahead and ask.

MICK: Go so.

MAIRTIN (*pause*): And ask do they cut the willies off and give them to tinkers?

MICK: Aye.

MAIRTIN (*pause*): I'll go so.

MICK: So go.

MAIRTIN: I'm going. I don't need you to tell me to be going.

> MAIRTIN *slowly idles off stage left.* MICK *smiles to himself when he's gone, then gets out of the grave he's in, having finished collecting its bones, lifts the sack out with him and puts it to one side. He idles over stage left to his wife's grave and looks down at it a while, hands in pockets. Enter the guard,* THOMAS HANLON, *stage right, in full uniform, sucking on, at intervals throughout, a cigarette and an asthma inhaler.*

THOMAS: You haven't started?

MICK: I haven't started.

THOMAS: What are you doing so?

MICK: I'm just looking at it.

THOMAS: Oh aye. No harm. I had some trouble out at the Riordans' hall is why I'm late. Two women fighting and one man.

MICK: Was the two women fighting the man or who was fighting who?

THOMAS: The two women was fighting among themselves and getting on fine when this oul fella butted in saying 'It's not right women fighting, break it up', and didn't the two of them deck him and take it in turns treading on him?

MICK: Good enough for him. What business was it of his them fighting? I like a good fight between women.

THOMAS: The same as that, I like a good fight between women, although I couldn't say that while on duty, like. We arrested the lot of them anyways. The oul fella couldn't believe it. Went crying he did. Crying and wouldn't stop crying. And Johnny Doyle said 'I'll give you a batter too if you don't stop', but even then he wouldn't stop.

MICK: Did he give him a batter so?

THOMAS: Ah no, now. There's no call to batter oul fellas, even if they're crying.

MICK: There's not I suppose.

THOMAS: Ah no. Sure we'll be oul fellas too someday.

MICK (pause): I'll get a start on this, so.

THOMAS: Go ahead for yourself, aye.

> MICK *starts digging up his wife's grave.* THOMAS *sits against the right-hand headstone and looks inside the black sack, grimacing a little.*

THOMAS: Awful morbid work this is, Mick.

MICK: It's work to be done.

THOMAS: Awful ghoulish though.

MICK: Work to be done it is. Isn't the space needed?

THOMAS: I'm certain there are other ways. Encouraging cremation is what the church should be. Not all this.

MICK: Who around here would go for cremation? No one.

THOMAS: It's got to be better than this every year.

MICK: Get onto them so. *(Pause.)* Don't you come across more morbid things than this in your work every day? People only minutes dead you come across, neverminding seven years.

THOMAS: When do I come across people only minutes dead?

MICK: Do you not? Oh. I thought the way you do talk about it, just like *Hill Street Blues* your job is. Bodies flying about everywhere.

THOMAS: I would *like* there to be bodies flying about everywhere, but there never is.

MICK: Go ahead up north so. You'll be well away. Hang about a bookies or somewhere.

THOMAS: Ah there's no detective work in that oul bullshit. Detective work I'm talking about. You know, like *Quincy*.

MICK: Oh, like *Quincy*. *(Pause.)* Have you never seen a dead body, so? A just dead body?

THOMAS: The only body I've ever seen was a fella in a block of flats the road to Shannon. The fattest bastard you've ever seen in your life. Tits like this. Sitting, no clothes, in his armchair. No clothes, now. Television still on. A heart attack, the doctor said. All well and good. He knows more than me. But I had meself a look in that fat man's fridge, now. A mighty fridge it was, six feet high. What was in there? A pot of jam and a lettuce. Eh? And nothing else. A pot of jam and a lettuce in the fridge of the fattest man you've ever seen in your life. Nothing suspicious in that? I pointed it out in my report to them, and they just laughed at me. And watching television stark naked too? Nothing suspicious in that?

MICK (*pause*): What time of year was it?

THOMAS: What time of year? I don't know . . .

MICK: If it was the height of summer, and he wasn't expecting any visitors, it might very well explain the stark naked.

THOMAS (*pause*): It might explain the stark naked, aye. It might not explain the complete absence of food in his six-foot fridge! Eh?

MICK: You have a point.

THOMAS: I have a point, aye. I know I have a point. The amount of food a fat fella eats? He won't get far on a lettuce and a pot of jam! Just laughed at me they did. (*Pause.*) Where's the young shite anyways?

MICK: Gone up to the church. I told him to ask the priest is it right the Church hands out the willies of the dead to passing tinker children to play with.

THOMAS: And he hasn't gone?

MICK: He has gone.

THOMAS: Oh he's as thick as five thick fellas, that fecker. What do they teach them in school now anyways?

MICK: I don't know what they teach them. Cooking cats they teach them.

THOMAS: Cooking cats, aye. No. A hamster it was.

MICK: It's the same difference, sure.

THOMAS: Pardon me?

MICK: It's the same difference, I said.

THOMAS: It's not the same difference at all, sure. A cat is one thing. A hamster is another.

MICK: Is it worth the argue, now?

THOMAS: I'm just saying, like. *(Pause.)* A fact is a fact, like. It's the same in detective work. No matter how small a detail may appear to be, you can't go lumping it with a bunch of other details like it's all the same thing. So you can't go lumping cats and hamsters together either. Things like that are the difference between solving and not solving an entire case, sure.

MICK: Oh aye, aye, they are, I suppose.

MICK *returns to his digging.*

THOMAS: They are. They certainly are. Oh aye. *(Pause.)* How far are you down?

MICK: I'm down a good way. Funny, this soil's easy digging . . .

MAIRTIN *returns, angry, rubbing his cheek.*

MAIRTIN: A back-fecking-hander the fecker gave me, you fecking bastard ya!

MICK *and* THOMAS *laugh.*

MAIRTIN: What the feck are yous laughing for, you feckers you?

THOMAS: Stop your cursing now, Mairtin. Not in the graveyard. Against God so it is.

MAIRTIN: Against God, is it?

THOMAS: It is.

MAIRTIN: Feck God so! And his mother too!

Both MICK *and* THOMAS *stop to chastise* MAIRTIN, THOMAS *standing.*

MICK: Hey . . . !!

THOMAS: Now, Mairtin, I'm liable to give you a batter meself if you go on like that, and a better batter it will be than the one you got from that biteen of a priest.

MAIRTIN: Ah, go to blazes with you.

THOMAS: A bloody better batter it will be.

MAIRTIN: Of course. Aren't the polis the experts at battering gasurs anyway? Don't you get a bonus for it?

MICK *continues digging.*

THOMAS: What gasurs do I ever batter?

MAIRTIN: Ray Dooley for a start-off, or if not you then your bastarding cohorts.

THOMAS: What about Ray Dooley?

MAIRTIN: Didn't he end up the County Hospital ten minutes after you arrested him?

THOMAS: He did, the pisshead, a broken toe. Kicking the cell door in and forgetting he had no shoes on him.

MAIRTIN: Aye, that's what *you* say. That's what *you* say.

THOMAS *(pause)*: Don't be cursing God in a graveyard, anyway, is what the crux of the matter is.

MAIRTIN: Aye, and don't be invading people's human rights is what the other crux of the matter is. The guards are there to serve the people, not the other way round, if you'd like to know.

THOMAS: You've been paying attention in Sociology class anyways, Mairtin.

MAIRTIN: I have.

THOMAS: That's a good thing. Is it still Miss Byrne with the mini-skirts teaches that?

MAIRTIN: I'm not bandying around pleasantries with the likes of you!

MICK: Get back to fecking work, so, and start filling that one in.

MAIRTIN tuts and goes to the right-hand grave with his shovel. He starts tipping the dirt back into it.

MAIRTIN *(to* THOMAS*):* I see you say nothing to him when he says 'feck' in the graveyard. Is it only kids, so you go shouting the odds with?

THOMAS: It is, aye. Only kids.

MAIRTIN: I know well it is.

THOMAS: I do like to specialise.

MAIRTIN: I know you do. *(Pause. Mumbling.)* Specialise me black arsehole.

As MAIRTIN *continues shovelling dirt at the grave's edge,* THOMAS *quietly walks up behind him and shoves him down into it.* MAIRTIN *yelps.* MICK *and* THOMAS *laugh, kicking dirt down onto him.* MAIRTIN *quickly clambers up from the rotten coffin underfoot.*

MAIRTIN: You're a fecking fecker, Thomas. And you're nothing else.

THOMAS (*laughing*): Haven't I told you, now, about your language?

MAIRTIN: I'm going the feck home.

THOMAS: You're not going the feck home either. I've told Dad to give you a batter himself if you're home before daybreak. So there you are.

MAIRTIN: You're always ganging up on me, the fecking two of ye.

THOMAS: Ah, the babby's going crying now. Go on and help Mick, whiny, or I'll tell oul Welsh to be docking your wages on you.

MAIRTIN (*pause*): Do you need help with the digging there, Mick?

MICK: No. Go on ahead with your filling in that one.

MAIRTIN *does so.* THOMAS *lights a cigarette.*

THOMAS (*pause*): Aren't you getting nervous there now, Mick? I'd be nervous, seeing me wife again after such a time.

MICK: What's to be nervous for?

MAIRTIN: Aye, what's to be nervous for?

THOMAS: Nothing at all, now.

MICK: Nothing at all is right.

THOMAS: Aye, now. Only I thought you might have some things on your mind might be making you nervous seeing your missus again.

MICK: What kind of things on me mind?

MAIRTIN: Aye, what kind of things on his mind?

THOMAS: I don't know, now. I have no idea at all. Just things on your mind, like.

MICK: I have no things on me mind.

THOMAS: Good-oh. I was just saying, like.

MICK: What things are you saying I have on me mind?

THOMAS: No things at all, sure. None at all. Just conversing we are.

MICK: Conversing me arse. Do you have something to say to me?

THOMAS: No, no, now . . .

MICK: Because if you do, go ahead and spit it out. Is it me drink-driving you're saying?

THOMAS: I was saying nothing, now, Mick.

MICK: Casting aspersions on me . . . ?

THOMAS: I was casting no aspersions at all . . .

MICK: The family of eejits and blackguards you come from?

MAIRTIN (pause): Who's an eejit and a blackguard? Is it me he's talking about, Thomas?

THOMAS: It is, aye.

MAIRTIN (*pause*): How do you know it's me he's talking about? It could've been you or Dad or anybody he was talking about.

THOMAS: Who were you talking about, Mick?

MICK: Him.

THOMAS (*to* MAIRTIN): See?

MAIRTIN: Ya feck!

THOMAS: Now, Mick, you've insulted poor wee Mairtin there, you've insulted family, such as it is, so now I have to go and say something insulting back to you. That is the way that these things operate.

MICK: You're the one who started with the insults.

THOMAS: No, Mick, no. I have to take you up on that. You're the one who started with the insults. I was the one who started with the vague insinuations.

MICK: It's the self-same thing.

THOMAS: Pardon me?

MICK: It's the self-same thing, I said.

THOMAS: It's not the self-same thing at all, and if you knew anything about the law then you'd know it's not the self-same thing. So now I have to turn me vague insinuations into something more of an insult, so then we'll all be quits . . .

MAIRTIN (*to* MICK): Your ma was a queer and your da was a queer and how they came up with you is a mystery of the Universe!

Both MICK *and* THOMAS *stare blankly at* MAIRTIN *for a few moments, who looks away, embarrassed. Pause.*

THOMAS: No, what I was going to say was . . . some insinuation along the lines of . . . not that I'm making any accusations, mind . . . but maybe your wife's head injuries all those years ago weren't especially conducive to only having been in a car crash at all, and maybe . . .

MICK *(angrily)*: All that came out at the time, Thomas Hanlon, and didn't the inquest shoot every word of it down!

THOMAS: Y'know, maybe she was already dead *before* you drove her into the wall, that kind of insinuation, like. But nothing harsher than that am I saying.

MICK: Take all of that back, Thomas Hanlon!

THOMAS: I'm only suggesting, now, like.

MICK: Take every word of it back, because if you make me get up out of this grave, now, polis or not . . .

THOMAS: You take eejit and blackguard back, so, and I'll be pleased to take it back.

MICK: You take your things back first.

THOMAS: No, now. You said your things first, so it's only fair you take them back first too.

MICK: There was no call for any of this.

THOMAS: I agree with you, like.

MICK: For any of these insults. *(Pause.)* I take eejit and blackguard back.

THOMAS: I take wife-butcherer back, so.

MAIRTIN *laughs loudly, half in surprise, half in pride, as* MICK *and* THOMAS *stare at each other.*

MAIRTIN: Is that all true?

MICK: A pure drink-driving it was, Thomas, and you know full well it was.

THOMAS: I *do* know full well it was, and I've taken me accusations back without reservation.

MAIRTIN: Is it true, Thomas?

THOMAS: Of course it's not true, Mairtin. Haven't I just said? I made up every word of it.

MAIRTIN *(confused)*: I thought you were saying it was true.

THOMAS: Not at all. A pure drink-driving is all it was, just like Mick says.

MICK *and* THOMAS *stare at each other a few seconds more, then* MICK *returns to his digging.*

MAIRTIN: Oh-h. I'm disappointed so.

THOMAS: Why are you disappointed, babby?

MAIRTIN: There you got me hoping I was working with a fella up and slaughtered his wife with an axe or something, when all it was was an oul cheap-ass drink-driving. Aren't they ten-a-penny? Wouldn't it be hard to find somebody round here who *hasn't* killed somebody drink-driving? Or if not a somebody then a heifer, or at least a dog. Didn't oul Marcus Rigby kill twins with his tractor, and him over seventy?

THOMAS: No, he did not.

MAIRTIN: Did he not? Who was it killed twins with his tractor so? It was someone.

THOMAS: No. That was just something I told you when you was twelve to mind you kept out of the road with your bicycle when you saw a tractor coming.

MAIRTIN (*pause*): There was no twins at all?

THOMAS: If you had any sense you'd have known when did ever twins live around here?

MAIRTIN: Twins come over from America I was thinking, to see where *The Quiet Man* was filmed and got lost.

THOMAS: You was thinking wrong, so. I only said twins to get you thinking if a tractor killed two gasurs it'd be twice as likely a tractor'd kill you, there only being one of you.

MAIRTIN (*angrily*): So all those years I drove me bicycle through hedgerows and banks of skitter and all on account of them poor mangled twins I had on me mind, and it was all for nothing?!

THOMAS (*laughing*): It was, indeed.

MAIRTIN: You're a bastard of a bastard of a bastard of a feck, Thomas Hanlon!

THOMAS: You're still alive anyways, is the main thing. Do you know how many boys the age of eight died falling into slurry tanks the last year in Ireland alone?

MAIRTIN: I don't! And I don't fecking care!

THOMAS: Fourteen. Fourteen of the poor gasurs.

MAIRTIN: Good! And let them die!

THOMAS: And drowning in slurry, Mairtin beag, isn't the nicest way to go out of this world. I'll tell you that for yourself.

MAIRTIN: Feck drowning in slurry, and feck their mothers too . . . !

MICK (interrupting): That's not true, now, is it, Thomas? The fourteen gasurs drowning in the slurry?

THOMAS: It is true, aye. (Pause.) Not altogether, mind . . .

MICK: No.

THOMAS: Not all in the one tank, now. Separately.

MICK: Separately. In different parts of the country, like, and at different times.

THOMAS: Aye. From the Central Office of Statistics this is. They have good statistics they do. More kids die in slurry tanks than die in combine harvesters. Only seven died in combine harvesters.

MICK: Of course. Because more people have slurry tanks than have combine harvesters.

THOMAS: That's true enough.

MICK: It's only rich people have combine harvesters. And their kids are less thick anyways.

THOMAS: Is right.

MICK: To go climbing in slurry you have to be thick.

THOMAS: You do.

MAIRTIN (angrily): It wasn't climbing in slurry this conversation was at all! This conversation was the lie about the dead twins!

As he speaks, THOMAS *pushes* MAIRTIN *over into the grave again and kicks dirt at him.*

THOMAS: Ah, shut your creeping bollocks about the dead twins, ya fecking oul shite-arse ya, and you're nothing else.

MAIRTIN: Kick dirt at me, is it?! And . . . and call me an oul shite-arse, is it?!

THOMAS: It is. You observed well.

MAIRTIN: We'll see about that so, you fecker . . .

THOMAS: Oh aye, now. The babby's angry . . .

MAIRTIN *starts clambering up out of the side of the grave to get at* THOMAS, *who takes his truncheon out in readiness. Just as* MAIRTIN *gets to his feet, the sound of* MICK'S *shovel splintering the rotten coffin lid under his feet is heard.*

MICK: I'm through to it.

MAIRTIN *and* THOMAS *stare at each other a moment, then forget their fight and go and stand over* MICK *at the grave.* MICK *crouches down, so he's almost out of sight, to pull up the rotten boards.*

THOMAS: Prepare yourself so, Mick, now. She'll be a shock to you.

MICK: The boards are . . . funny. The boards are already broke open, or is that just the rot, now?

MICK *throws a couple of bits of rotten board away.*

THOMAS: Dig some more of that dirt off there, Mick.

MICK *takes his shovel and scrapes some more of the dirt from the coffin. After a few seconds, his scraping starts becoming more frantic.*

MICK: What's the . . . ? What's the . . . ?

THOMAS: Is she . . . ?

MAIRTIN: This is a peculiar business.

MICK *throws the shovel away and ducks down into the grave again, this time desperately scraping the dirt away with his bare hands.*

MICK (*frantic*): Where is she . . . ?! Where is she . . . ?!

THOMAS (*quietly*): Is she not . . . ?

MICK (*shouting, voice almost breaking*): She's not there!

His scraping ceases. Pause. He stands back up, dirty and bedraggled, looking down into the grave numbly.

(*Quietly.*) She's not there.

Pause. Blackout.

Scene Three

*Night, a day or two later. Set the same as in Scene One.
Three skulls and their sets of bones lie on the table in front
of* MAIRTIN *who stares dumbly down at them, swaying,
drunk, blowing bubbles. He has a mallet in one hand and
a quarter-empty bottle of poteen in the other, from which
he takes disgusted sips every now and then.* MICK *can be
heard rummaging through a toolbox offstage. He is also
drunk.*

MICK (*off*): There's another one here somewhere I know.

MAIRTIN: What do you be wanting an oul woody hammer
for, Mick, now?

MICK: They do call them mallets.

MAIRTIN: Ohh. (*Pause.*) Skulls do be more scary on your
table than they do in their coffin. Why? I don't know
why. Some reason now.

MICK: Are you getting scared, you wee pup?

MAIRTIN: I'm not getting sacred at all. All right I'm getting a
bit scared. You won't be leaving me on me own more
long?

MICK: The minute I find this feck I'll be with you. No chance of you helping me look.

MAIRTIN *(absently)*: No. *(Pause.)* Weren't they terrible heathens whoever pinched your missus on you?

MICK: They were. And if I ever get me hands on the fecks, then we'd see.

MAIRTIN: What would you do to them, Mick? Would you give them a kick?

MICK: It would be worse than a kick.

MAIRTIN: Would you peg stones at them?

MICK: Worse than stones it'd be.

MAIRTIN: Peg . . . biteens'a . . . rocks . . .

MICK: You wouldn't have heard tell of who took her, Mairtin? Not one of your oul mates, I'm thinking?

MAIRTIN: None of my mates. What would one of my mates be wanting with your oul missus? My mates don't be fooling with dead missuses.

MICK: And can we rule you off the list of suspects too?

MAIRTIN: I'm on no list of suspects. If I was to be digging up your missus it's good money I'd be wanting for the job, the same as you, cash in hand. Maybe it was a set of tinkers dug her up on you.

MICK: What would tinkers be wanting with her?

MAIRTIN: I don't know. Maybe they were expecting another praitie blight and felt like something to be munching on ahead of time. Not that there'd be much to munch on with your missus. No willy anyways. As far as I know anyways, I didn't know the woman. I still can't believe that about them willies. That's an awful thing.

MICK: Found the feck!

MICK *enters, a half-empty bottle of poteen in one hand, a mallet in the other, which he shows to* MAIRTIN.

MAIRTIN: What will you be playing so, Mick? That oul game with the hoops and the sticks they do play in England with the hoops and the sticks and the balls they do play in England, what's it called, with the hoops and the sticks? They do play it in England. It has a 'c.'

MICK: Are you looking in me eyes now, Mairtin?

MAIRTIN: What eyes?

MICK: *My* eyes.

MAIRTIN: Aye, your eyes. *Croquet!*

MICK: Did you have anything to do with my wife going missing?

MAIRTIN: Eh?

MICK: Did you have anything to do with my wife going missing?

MAIRTIN: No.

MICK *keeps staring at* MAIRTIN *for a long time, as* MAIRTIN *sways slightly but returns the stare.*

MICK: You have looked me in the eyes and I believe you now, Mairtin. I do apologise for even asking you.

MAIRTIN: Good-oh.

MICK *shakes* MAIRTIN *by the hand and walks over to the table.*

MICK: Are these skulls still scaring you?

MAIRTIN: I'm less scared now but don't be leaving me on me own again with them. When they get me on me own they do go smiling at me. Especially that one.

MICK: Shall we be teaching them a lesson then so?

MAIRTIN: Sure you can't teach skulls lessons. They have no brain to be sticking the . . . lesson . . .

MICK: Knowledge?

MAIRTIN: Knowledge. They have no brain to be sticking the lesson through the holes knowledge into.

MICK: This is the only lesson skulls be understanding.

He brings the mallet crashing down on the skull nearest to him, shattering it, spraying pieces of it all over the room.

He won't be smiling no more.

MAIRTIN: You've buggered him to skitter!

MICK: I have. Not skitter enough.

MICK *starts smashing the skull into even smaller pieces and stamping on the bits that have fallen on the floor.* MAIRTIN *stares at him dumbfounded.*

MAIRTIN: Ease them in the lake you said.

MICK: In front of the fat one I said, aye. Batter the shite out of them is nearer the mark. And why not? If it's whispering about me they're going to be through the years, what more should they expect when they wind up in my hands than batter?

MAIRTIN: Nothing more.

MICK: Nothing more is right.

MAIRTIN: May I be having a batter, Mick? Ah let me now.

MICK: Why else have I invited you here with a hammer in your hand?

MAIRTIN: I can? Ohh jeebies . . . Goodbye Daniel Faragher. You've been smiling at me long enough, boy.

MAIRTIN *takes a little run-up and starts smashing another of the skulls and its bones to pieces. The smashing continues more or less unabated by at least one of the men throughout most of the rest of the scene.*

MICK: That one's Biddy Curran, not Dan Faragher at all.

MAIRTIN: Biddy Curran, ya currant bun, ya . . .

MICK: She was a fat oul bitch.

MAIRTIN: She's thin enough now, God bless her. And getting more thin.

MICK: The middle one's Dan, and Dan's mine.

MICK *starts smashing the middle skull.*

MAIRTIN: Ar, you've done two and I've only done one, Mick, ya snatching feck.

MICK: Don't be crying, Mairtin. And haven't you had half a bottle of poteen off me today if I'm such a snatching feck?

MAIRTIN: I have. *(Drinks.)* You're not a snatching feck at all. You're a generous man.

MICK: You can join in with Dan's bones if you like.

MAIRTIN: I'll be taking a pop at Biddy Curran's pelvis and then I'll see how I'm feeling.

MICK: Good-oh.

MAIRTIN: Should you not be putting a whatyoucall down to be catching them?

MICK: What matter?

MAIRTIN: Or a thing?

MICK: If you'll not be liking my skull-battering ways you can be off with you.

MAIRTIN: Your ways is fine indeed.

MICK: I do have a dustpan and brush.

MAIRTIN: I was thinking. Goodbye Biddy Curran or whatever it is your name is. You're all mixed up now anyways, you poor feck you.

MICK: Don't be cursing now, Mairtin.

MAIRTIN: I won't be.

MICK: Not when you're handling the departed, now.

MAIRTIN: This is more fun than hamster-cooking!

MICK: It is. Or if it is I don't know. I've never cooked hamsters.

MAIRTIN: I've only cooked one hamster. It's not all it's cracked up to be. You stick him in alive and he comes out dead. The feck hardly squeals . . . I mean, the fella hardly squeals. If the oven had had a see-through door it would've been more fun, but it didn't, it had an ordinary door. My mistake was not planning ahead. I was egged on. But this is more fun. Is skull-hammering more fun than wife-into-wall-driving, Mick?

MICK: Oh Mairtin, you're getting a bit near to the mark there, boy.

MAIRTIN: Oh I am. When I drink I do get awful stupid. I apologise, Mick.

MICK: I accept your apology, Mairtin. Seeing as you're drunk as Jaysus.

MAIRTIN: I *am* drunk as Jaysus. But I'll be putting me head in a bucket of water when I get home and I'll be fine then. I do that of a Saturday night I do, and me dad does never twig I've been drinking.

MICK: Be remembering to take your head out of the bucket afterwards is the main thing.

MAIRTIN: I know. Else you'd go drowning.

MICK: Is right.

MAIRTIN *stops hammering abruptly, to launch into his story, and* MICK *stops quickly so, to listen.*

MAIRTIN: Did my brother ever tell you the drunk out in Salthill, lay down on the floor to sleep, and where was his head resting? His head was resting in a potty of wee. Drowned he did! On wee! Eh?

MICK: On wee, was it?

MAIRTIN: Drowned on wee. What a way to go, eh?

MICK: Was it his own wee?

Slight pause.

MAIRTIN: I don't know if it was his own wee or not. And I don't care. He drowned on wee is all I'm saying.

MICK: No, now. A fact like that is very important, now. Your brother would be the first to agree.

MAIRTIN (*pause*): Now that I think of it, I think my brother *did* want to launch an investigation into the matter, but they wouldn't let him. But I don't know if it was whose wee it was was what aroused his suspicions or not. Sure, a pig that smelt would arouse that bastard's suspicions. Thinks he's Starsky and Hutch. (*Pause.*) I, for one, would rather drown on me own wee than on anybody else's. Though I'd rather not drown on wee at all!

MICK: I had three uncles drowned on sick.

MAIRTIN (*pause*): But, sure, drowned on sick is nothing to go shouting about. Doesn't everybody drown on sick?

MICK: Three uncles, now I'm saying.

MAIRTIN: Three uncles or no. Drowned on sick is ten-a-penny now, Mick. A million have drowned on sick. Oul black fella. Jimi Hendrix. Drowned on wee I'm talking about. Drowned on wee you have to go out of your way. Drowned on sick you don't. And of course. Sick is there in your gob already. Wee is nowhere near.

MICK: If it's drunk you are and you go to bed and you fear you may be sick, this is what you should do . . .

He lies down flat on his belly on the floor, his face to one side.

Lay down flat on your belly or on your side, your face turned to the side of the pillow. Or throw the pillow away completely would be the best thing.

MAIRTIN: I don't need advice from you, Mick Dowd, on not drowning on sick. I know well.

MICK: Like this, now.

MAIRTIN: I know like that, and your floor is filthy.

MICK: This is what I always remember on going to bed, no matter how much of a sup I've had, this is what I always remember *(Almost tearfully.)* in mind of me three poor uncles, were young men.

MAIRTIN: Get up anyways, now, because it wasn't sick was the subject at all. You do always be changing the subject on me. Wee was the subject.

MICK *(getting up)*: Three uncles, I'm saying.

MAIRTIN: I know, three uncles.

MICK: And one of them in America.

MAIRTIN: In America? I suppose people do drown on their sick in America too. Oh of course.

MICK: In Boston Massachusetts.

MAIRTIN: In Boston Massachusetts?

MICK: In Boston Massachusetts. He did drown on his sick.

MAIRTIN: I suppose at least he'd travelled. (*Pause.*) Good-oh.

The two almost simultaneously begin smashing up the bones again.

MICK: We should have music as we're doing this.

MAIRTIN (*blankly*): Music, music . . .

MICK: Music to hammer dead fellas to. I have a Dana record somewhere . . .

MAIRTIN: Put Dana on so.

MICK *puts on 'All Kinds of Everything' by Dana.*

MICK: I didn't think young people liked Dana nowadays.

MAIRTIN: They may not but I do. I've liked Dana since I was a child. If I met Dana I'd give her a kiss.

MICK: She wouldn't be kissing you, ya get.

MAIRTIN: For why?

MAIRTIN *stops hammering, looking sad and serious.* MICK *stops and looks at him.*

MICK: Why wouldn't Dana be kissing you?

MAIRTIN: Aye.

MICK (*pause*): Well maybe she would, now.

MAIRTIN: On the lips.

MICK (*shrugging*): Maybe she would.

MAIRTIN: Although she's a born-again Christian now.

MICK: Honestly, Mairtin, I'd avoid her.

MICK *starts hammering again, and after a few seconds* MAIRTIN *joins him.*

MAIRTIN *(pause)*: Would you be hammering your missus's bones with equal fervour were she here, Mick?

MICK: I wouldn't be. I'd have some respect.

MAIRTIN: Maybe a favour it was they did you so, the fellas went and stole her on you?

MICK: No favour was it to me, and if I had the feckers here, then you'd be seeing some fancy skull-battering. I'll tell you that. Battered to dust they would be!

MAIRTIN: Good enough for them, the morbid oul fecks. And not only stealing your missus then, if that weren't enough, but to go pinching the locket that lay round her neck too, a locket that wouldn't fetch you a pound in the Galway pawn, I'd bet.

MICK *has stopped hammering on the locket's first mention and stepped back a pace, staring at* MAIRTIN *whose hammering continues unabated, entirely unaware of his faux-pas.*

MICK: The rose locket, was it?

MAIRTIN: The rose locket, aye, with the picture of you. What use would the fecks have in taking that, other than just to taunt you?

MICK *sits down in the armchair, the mallet in his lap, still staring at* MAIRTIN, *who continues ahead with the skulls.*

MAIRTIN: The miserable heathen gets, and that's all they are. It was probably the same ones stole me *Star Wars* men on me when I was four, when I left them out in the rain. It was Han and Luke and . . . was it Chewie? No, I didn't have Chewie. It was Han and Luke and some other one they had off me . . . Princess Leia! Aye, and them are the three best ones in *Star Wars*. You can't play *Star Wars* without them. Look at you sitting there! Be getting back to work you, ya slack feck ya, or I'll have a word with oul Welsh Walsh to be docking your wages on you. Welsh.

MICK: In a minute now, Mairtin. I've to sit down and be having a think a minute.

MAIRTIN *(stopping hammering)*: That's what all the clever kids at school do do is sit down and be having a think, when it's out in the yard playing football they should be, and getting some sun on their arms. You can't budge the freckle-faced fecks, not even with a dig. *(Pause.)* Ah good luck to them, they're not harming anyone. Why should I be ordering them about and giving them digs? They've every right to be sitting. *(Pause.)* I do get in an awful happy mood when it's out of me brains I am, Mick.

MICK: I can see.

MAIRTIN: I could kiss fools and feck dogs. *(Pause.)* Have we done enough hammering for the meantime so?

MICK: We have.

MAIRTIN: What's next on the agenda?

MICK: Be picking up a few of the big lumps, there, and be putting them in the sack.

MAIRTIN *does so, drunkenly.*

MAIRTIN: Ah there's too many of the bastards to be picking up. You should get a hoover.

MICK: Just a few more of the big ones will do us.

MAIRTIN: I was promised a dustpan and brush a while back. I see that promise proved untrue. Now what?

MICK *(standing)*: Now we'll be driving them out to the lake to be starting the disposing.

MAIRTIN: With a string of prayers said over them, Mick?

MICK: With a string of prayers said over them. I'll be getting me car out now, unless I don't suppose you'd want to be driving, Mairtin?

MAIRTIN: Ah you wouldn't let me be driving, would ya?

MICK: If you're not up to the job, no I wouldn't be.

MAIRTIN: I'd be up to the job, Mick! I'd be up to the job!

MICK: You're not a tadeen over the limit, now?

MAIRTIN: I'm not near the limit, sure. I've had a bare sip. Oh let me be driving, Mick. Please now.

Pause. MICK *takes his car keys out of his pocket and tosses them to* MAIRTIN, *who fumbles them at length and drops them, then drunkenly picks them back up off the floor.*

MAIRTIN: Oh jeebies, this has turned into a great oul night. Driving and drinking and skull-battering . . .

MAIRTIN *dashes out through the front door, leaving his sack behind him.*

MICK: Be bringing your bag of skulleens now, Mairtin!

Pause. MAIRTIN *returns slowly, smiling, and picks up the sack.*

MAIRTIN: I'd forget me head if it wasn't screwed up. *On.* Me mam does say 'You'd forget your head you would, Mairtin.' I say oh aye.

He exits with sack.

(Off.) I'll be sure and remember to be putting me seatbelt on too, Mick, knowing your track record.

Sound of MAIRTIN *laughing, off.*

MICK *(quietly)*: Be doing what you like, ya feck . . .

He picks up his mallet and rolls it around in his hand a little.

It'll make no difference in the end.

He exits briskly, bringing the mallet with him and turning the lights off behind him, as the sound of a car starting up is heard.

SCENE FOUR

MICK *enters, turns lights on. His shirt is covered in blood. He wipes some blood off his mallet and lays it on the table, then brushes the bone fragments littering the floor into the next room. He sits in his armchair when finished. There is a knock at the door.* MICK *lets* MARYJOHNNY *in.*

MARY: Mick.

MICK: Maryjohnny.

MARY: Cold.

MICK: I suppose it's cold.

MARY: Oh, now, it's cold, Mick.

MICK: Well, it's *night* I suppose.

MARY: Oh it's night, aye.

MICK: I suppose a sup would you be after?

MARY: Ah only if you're having one, Mick, now.

MICK *pours them two glasses.*

148

MARY: I've just come from the bingo.

MICK: Oh aye, and how many times tonight did you win?

MARY: Only three times tonight, Mick. One of me fluorescent pens ran out on me.

MICK: Uh-huh, that's always the worry with fluorescent pens. You had a bad night of it so.

MARY: Two free goes on the bumpy slides at the Leisureland swimming is all they gave me. I won't get much use out of them. *(Pause.)* You wouldn't want them, Mick?

MICK: I wouldn't, Mary. I was never a man for bumpy slides. Never saw the sense in them.

MARY: I'll give them to Mairtin or someone so. Is Mairtin able to swim?

MICK *wipes some of the blood from himself.*

MICK: I'd bet money against it.

MARY: What's all that on you, Mick? Out painting have you been?

MICK: I have, aye. I've been out painting red things.

MARY: That'll stain.

MICK: Ah it's just an oul work-shirt, Maryjohnny. What harm?

MARY: No harm. *(Pause.)* I heard tell of your Oona going missing on you, Mick. That was a terrible thing. If you can't be let rest when it's seven years dead you are, when can you be let rest.

MICK: You can never be let rest.

MARY: I couldn't bear to think of anyone running off with my bones when I'm dead.

MICK: No one'll run off with your bones, Maryjohnny. Sure, they'd need a small truck to begin with.

MARY: A small truck for why?

MICK: No why. Just a biteen big-boned sometimes you do seem.

MARY: I'm not big-boned. I'm just a bit fat is all.

MICK: A bit fat, oh aye, aye. A bit fat indeed.

MARY: It's a peculiar mood tonight you're in, Mick.

MICK: It is. It must be them paint fumes or something.

MARY *(pause)*: Did you hear Ray Dooley's lost his tour guide job?

MICK: I did. Sure, if you go pegging shite at Americans you're bound to lose your tour guide job.

MARY: You are.

MICK: And cracking Vietnam jokes then.

MARY: Off to Boston for his brother's wedding next month he is.

MICK: Next month, is it? That wasn't a very long engagement. Me and Oona five years we were engaged, and it was five years we well needed. To get to know each other's faults and the like, y'know, and to accept them then.

MARY: What was Oona's biggest fault, Mick?

MICK: Oona didn't have big faults really. She just had little faults. Niggly things, y'know? She'd never wrap up cheese properly. Y'know, when she was finished with it. She'd just leave it lying about, letting the air get to it. The same with bread. She'd never wrap up bread properly. Y'know, like after she'd made a sandwich or the like. And she was terrible at scrambled eggs, and I don't know why, because scrambled eggs are easy to do. Oona's scrambled eggs'd come out either grey or burned.

MARY: You don't miss her so.

MICK: I *do* miss her. I mean, that scrambled egg business wasn't really a big thing. We'd just avoid having scrambled eggs, y'know? *(Pause.)* I miss the talk of her. Oona could fill the house with talk. And she'd always stand up for me against people. Y'know, in a fight or something, or if people were saying things agin me. She'd've been the first to defend me if she heard the town was saying I murdered her on purpose.

MARY: It's a shame she's dead so. *(Pause.)* I wonder who it was took her?

MICK: Uh-huh?

THOMAS *knocks and enters, carrying a small bag.*

MARY: Evening, Thomas. Cold.

THOMAS: What are you doing up here?

MARY: I was passing on me way from the bingo.

THOMAS: I thought I told Father Welsh to bar you from the bingo.

MARY: You did but Father Welsh reinstated me to the bingo.

THOMAS: So he countermanded official police orders, did he? I'll have to be looking into that one. You run along home now, Gran. I want to speak to Mick alone.

MARY: I've only just got here, sure.

THOMAS: I don't care if you've only just got here. That's an official police order, I'm saying.

MARY: Don't you go official police ordering me, Thomas Hanlon, the number of times I wiped the dribbling skitter off the bare babby's backside of ya.

THOMAS: *Please*, Gran.

MARY: I'll go when I've finished me sup and not before.

MICK: What would you want to be speaking to me alone for anyways?

THOMAS: Oh nothing terrible important really. Just I'd like you to write out and sign a little confession for me, that's all. Just a weeny little confession, like.

MICK: A confession to what?

THOMAS *takes a skull with a large forehead-crack out of his bag.*

THOMAS: A confession to the murdering be blunt instrument, or be some sort of instrument, of your late wife, Mrs Oona Margaret Dowd.

THOMAS *gestures to the skull crack.*

MARY: No . . . !

MICK: Oh. Okay so.

THOMAS: Hah?

MICK: Okay, I said. Do ya have a pen?

THOMAS (*checks himself*): I don't. Don't you have one?

MICK *looks for a pen.*

MICK: I have one somewhere, I know.

MARY (*takes out bingo pens*): I have me bingo pens. They're fluorescent but they don't all work.

THOMAS: Sure fluorescent pens are no good for filling out confessions, sure!

MARY: A yalla one?

THOMAS: No. 'A yalla one', Jesus.

MICK (*finding pen*): Here, me lucky lotto pen. Now, what exactly do you want me to be saying, Thomas?

THOMAS: Well, the *truth*, Mick.

MICK: Oh, the truth, aye. Fair enough.

MICK *writes out his confession on two pieces of paper* THOMAS *gives him, as* MARY *picks the skull up.*

MARY: It's true? (*Pause.*) I had always prayed only fool gossiping is all it ever was. If I had known that . . .

MICK: If you had known that you'd still've come up cadging booze off me all these years, ya cheapskate fecking lump.

THOMAS: Don't you go calling my granny a cheapskate fecking lump, ya murdering oul ghoul, ya.

MICK: Murdering oul what ya?

THOMAS: Ghoul, ghoul.

MICK: Oh, ghoul. I thought you said 'whore'.

THOMAS: And don't go criticising me pronunciation either!

MICK: *(to* MARY*)*: You just put my wife's skull down now you, you and your fluorescent fecking pens. Look at as many fluorescent pens she has, Thomas, when bingo's supposed to be a bit of fun and a bit of fun to raise a few bob for them poor oul fecks in Africa. Out the mouths of starving darkies Maryjohnny rips her bingo winnings, but I see you don't go getting her confessing.

MARY: Isn't it better to starve darkies than to murder missuses?

MICK: Not at all is it better, and put my Oona down now, you, I've told you once. I don't want the pooh-stench of your manky hands grubbing all over her.

MARY *puts skull down and continues drinking.* MICK *writes.*

MICK: Where was it you found her, Thomas?

THOMAS: Down the bottom of our fields I found her.

MICK: The bottom of yere fields, oh aye. Down beside the bones of that dead cow Mairtin was telling us about the other day, I'll bet. The one he said wandered in and fell down dead, when doesn't the world and his wife know he dragged that cow screaming from Pato Dooley's place and hit it with a brick, and it's only as easy-going as Pato is he never pressed charges.

THOMAS: That's only circumstantial evidence.

MICK: No, that's only *hearsay* evidence.

THOMAS: Feck I'm always getting them two beggars mixed up. What harm? It isn't knowing the difference between hearsay and circumstantial evidence that makes you a great copper. No. Detective work it is, and going hunting down clues, and never letting a case drop no matter what the odds stacked against you, no matter how many years old.

MARY: Like *Petrocelli*.

THOMAS: Like *Petrocelli* is right, Gran, and the first thing I do when they promote me is reopen the case of that lettuce and jam man I was telling you about, 'cos I can't sleep nights sometimes thinking of that poor fella's murder going four years unsolved, as cold and alone in his big fat grave he lies.

MICK: And the fella who drowned on wee is another.

THOMAS: And the fella who drowned on wee is another. I may bring a urine expert in on that one.

MICK: What's another word for 'convulse'? I've used 'convulse' once and I don't want to be repeating meself.

THOMAS *(thinking)*: Convulse, convulse, convulse . . . Spasm.

MICK: Spasm, spasm, spasm . . . Good one. *(Writes.)*

THOMAS: I have a great vocabulary me, I do, oh aye. *(Pause.)* Are you nearly done?

MICK: I'm nearly done, all right.

MARY: Poor Oona. Why did you kill her, Mick? Sure, bad scrambled eggs is no just cause to butcher your wife.

MICK: I know it's not, Mary, and do you want to hear something funny? I *didn't* butcher my wife. Just like for seven long years I've been saying I didn't butcher my wife. I never butchered anybody 'til tonight.

He gives his confession to THOMAS, *who reads through it at speed.*

A pure, drink-driving was all my Oona was, as all along I've said, but if it's a murderer ye've always wanted living in yer midst, ye can fecking have one.

THOMAS: D'you think I'm going to believe this pile of fecking bull? Down the disco with Ray Dooley tonight Mairtin is, and nowhere but the disco.

MICK: But, sure, if down the disco Mairtin was, how would I have ended up with his bastard brains dripping down the bloody front of me?

MARY: No . . . !

MICK: D'you see how great a copper he is, Maryjohnny, with his skulls and his solving and his lettuces in empty fridges, yet doesn't bat an eye at a blood-soaked man standing whap-bang in front of the feck-brained fool . . .

THOMAS: You killed him?

MICK: I did, aye. His body's hanging halfway out the windscreen of me Anglia a mile away there.

THOMAS *dives for* MICK, *knocking him off his chair and strangling him on the floor,* MICK *barely defending himself.*

MARY: Leave him, Thomas, leave him! Thomas!

MAIRTIN *enters behind her, somewhat concussed, a big bloody crack down the centre of his forehead, dripping onto his shirt. He watches the fight a while,* MARY *noticing him after a few seconds, confused.*

MAIRTIN: What are them two gobshites up to?

THOMAS *stops strangling* MICK. *Both stand and stare at* MAIRTIN.

MAIRTIN: What are ye's feckers looking at? Ye's *fellas* looking at, I mean?

THOMAS *examines* MAIRTIN's *wound.* MARY *sits, refilling drink.*

MARY: How are you, Mairtin?

MAIRTIN: I'm fine, Gran, although a biteen of a headache I do have, aye. What are you doing pawing at me, you?

THOMAS *rubs* MAIRTIN's *face gently.*

THOMAS: We have you now, Michael Dowd. We have you now.

THOMAS *takes his handcuffs out and goes to* MICK.

MAIRTIN: Have him for what?

THOMAS: Have him for ramming a mallet through the poor brains of you.

MAIRTIN: A mallet? What are you talking about, sure? A pure drink-driving is all this was.

THOMAS: Hah?

MICK: Hah?

MAIRTIN: A pure drink-driving is all this was. What would Mick want to go malleting my poor brains for? Mick likes me an awful lot, don't you, Mick?

MICK: I do, Mairtin. Sure I think you're a great fella.

MAIRTIN: See, Thomas? Mick thinks I'm a great fella.

Behind THOMAS's *back,* MICK *picks up the confession and sets it alight. It slowly burns as* THOMAS *questions* MAIRTIN.

THOMAS: Listen, Mairtin, concussed is all you are now, and who wouldn't be . . .

MAIRTIN: I'm not at all concussed. It'd take more than a major car-crash to concuss me, I'll tell ya.

THOMAS: But didn't he just sign a confession saying he hacked through the drunken skull of ya?

MAIRTIN: Did ya, Mick?

MICK: No, no, I didn't, Mairtin.

MAIRTIN: There you go.

THOMAS: What d'you mean you didn't? Don't I have the fecking thing right here . . . ?

THOMAS *turns to see the last corner of the confession burning to ash.*

MICK: You've cocked it up again, haven't ya?

THOMAS: Mairtin? Listen to me. You're going to come down to the station with me, now, and you're going to swear out how Mick it was tried to kill you tonight . . .

MAIRTIN: Oh Jesus, can't you just leave poor Mick alone and in peace, you, *McMillan and Wife*?

THOMAS: Don't keep calling me *McMillan and Wife*, I've told you twenty fecking times!

MAIRTIN: If he said he didn't kill his missus that's good enough for me, and let it rest.

THOMAS: What are you on his fecking side for?!

MAIRTIN: Well why wouldn't I be on his fecking side, when it's me own blackguard brother I catch carving a hole in Mick's missus's skull there, the day after you'd dug her up on him.

THOMAS: Shut up about that digging . . . !

MAIRTIN: I won't shut up about that digging and I'll tell you why I won't shut up about that digging! Because not even a fecking pound would the Galway pawn give me for that rose locket, and you said it'd get me at least ten.

He gives MICK *the locket.*

Only gave me that to shut me up, he did, Mick, but I realise that'd be nothing more than stealing from ya, and not only stealing from ya but stealing from the poor dead wife of ya, and anyways the fella in the pawn said it was just a piece of shite not worth pissing on, so it's no great loss, ya know what I mean, like?

THOMAS: Are you finished, Mairtin?

MAIRTIN *(pause. Confused)*: Am I Finnish?

THOMAS: Are you *finished*, I said.

MAIRTIN: Oh, am I finished? *(Thinks a while.)* No I'm not finished, Mr high-and-mighty detective bollocks. Heh, detective me arse, when the whole of Leenane knows you'd have trouble arresting a shop-lifting child, if the child confessed with the chocolate round his gob. Or if you did arrest him you'd arrest him for killing the Kennedys.

THOMAS: Is that right?

MAIRTIN: It is. Sure it's only 'cos you're so good at helping kids across the road that you're even tolerated in this job.

THOMAS: You're finished now, are ya?

MAIRTIN: I'm finished for the minute, aye, but I may be thinking up some more insults for ya in a whileen once I get me breath back.

THOMAS: But for the time being you're finished?

MAIRTIN: For the time being I'm finished, aye. Sure haven't I just said five times?

THOMAS: Good-oh.

THOMAS *smashes* MAIRTIN *twice across the head with the mallet,* MAIRTIN *collapsing to the floor.*

MARY: Thomas!

MICK *forcibly restrains* THOMAS *from hitting* MAIRTIN *any more.*

MICK: Leave him, Thomas, Christ! Thomas!

MAIRTIN (*dazed*): What did he do that fer?

THOMAS *stares at* MICK *blankly a while, sucking a second on his inhaler,* MICK *still holding him by the arms.*

THOMAS: I think . . . I think . . . I think they're never going to promote me.

MICK *lets* THOMAS *go.* MAIRTIN *has crawled onto a chair. In a blank daze,* THOMAS *caresses* MAIRTIN's *cheek, then gently touches his bloody head.*

MAIRTIN (*quietly, worried*): Are you all right there, Tom?

THOMAS *nods blankly.*

THOMAS: I'll get you for all this someday, Mick Dowd. On me own soul I swear it.

MICK: Good luck so.

THOMAS *nods, glances at the skull and at* MICK, *then exits.* MICK *sits with his wife's skull in his hands.* MARY *dabs at* MAIRTIN's *bloody head with a hanky,* MAIRTIN *yelping slightly in pain.*

MAIRTIN: Ar Gran, ya bitch!

MARY *tuts.*

MAIRTIN: Ar Gran ya eejit, I meant. There'd better be none of your mouldy oul snot on that hanky now, Gran.

MARY: There's not, Mairtin. This is just me hanky for show.

MAIRTIN: Your hanky for show? Uh-huh?

He gives MICK *a look as if* MARY *is mad.*

D'ya hear this one?

MICK: I think maybe to hospital you should be going for yourself, now, Mairtin. A bang on the head can be awful serious if not looked at.

MAIRTIN: Ar hospitals are for poofs, sure.

MICK: Hospitals aren't for poofs. They let anybody in.

MAIRTIN: For poofs and for lesbos who can't take a middling dig.

MARY *tuts.*

MAIRTIN: Wha? 'Lesbos' isn't swearing.

MARY: Is it not?

MAIRTIN: No. It's short for lesbians, y'know.

MARY: Oh.

MAIRTIN: 'Lesbos'. Y'know, like Mona McGhee in me school with the beard. *(Pause.)* Five times I've asked that bitch out and she still won't go.

MICK: There's nothing the matter with lesbians, Mairtin. They're doing no harm to anybody.

MAIRTIN: They're not, I suppose. And they're great at tennis. Em, you can leave me now, Gran. You're sort of getting on me nerves now, so you are.

MARY *stops attending to* MAIRTIN *and watches* MICK *with skull a while.*

MAIRTIN: I suppose that'd be your missus, would it, Mick?

MICK: It would.

MAIRTIN: Uh-huh. Has she changed much since last you saw her?

MICK *(pause)*: She has, Mairtin.

MAIRTIN: Oh aye, it's been seven years, I suppose.

MARY *(pause)*: Do you like bumpy slides, Mairtin?

MAIRTIN: Bumpy slides? Where the hell did bumpy bloody slides come from?

MARY: I won two goes on the bumpy slides at Leisureland if you'd want to go.

MAIRTIN: You won't catch me going on the bumpy slides with you, missus. I'd look a pure fool.

MARY: No, you could bring somebody else, I'm saying.

She gives MAIRTIN *the tickets.*

MAIRTIN: Oh. Aye. Thank you, Gran. Maybe Mona'd want to go. Heh, this has been a great oul day, this has. Drinking and driving and bumpy slides, and that oul battering them skulls to skitter was the best part of the whole day.

MARY *stares at* MICK *sternly.*

MAIRTIN: Would you need any help in giving your Oona a batter, Mick, or will you be handling that one yourself, now.

MICK: I'll be handling this one meself, Mairtin.

MAIRTIN: Good-oh.

MICK: And I'll be sending you a bill for the damage to me Anglia before the week's out.

MAIRTIN: Ar that's not fair, Mick.

MICK: Well life's not fair, Mairtin.

MAIRTIN (*confused slightly*): It *is* fair. I like it anyways.

He gets to his feet and is overcome with dizziness. He sways around the room on weak legs and manages not to collapse only by clinging on to a wall.

Em, I think I might pop into that hospital after all. A biteen dizzy I am. I'll be seeing ye.

MICK: Be seeing you, Mairtin.

MAIRTIN *(pause)*: Be seeing you, Gran, I said!

MARY: Be seeing you, Mairtin.

MAIRTIN: Jeez, *deaf*.

> MAIRTIN *takes a deep breath then staggers across the room, swaying, just making it out through the door, which he pulls behind him.*

MARY: So you do hammer the bones to skitter so.

MICK: Tonight was the first time ever that hammering happened, Maryjohnny, and only because wasn't I pure upset at Oona going missing on me . . .

MARY: And you expect me to believe you, the lies you never stop spouting?

MICK: What lies?

MARY: A fool could see Mairtin's injuries were no accident.

MICK: And, sure, didn't I admit that one outright, and sign a confession to the fact? How was that a lie?

MARY: And the lies o'er your poor Oona's dying then.

MICK: Oh you're still not going on about that fecking one, are ya? I have never lied o'er Oona dying. Never once.

MARY: Oh no? I must've been mistaken what I saw that night so, as along the two of ye drove.

MICK: What did you see? There was nothing to see.

MARY: Oh I suppose there was nothing to see, now.

MICK: If you've something to say to me, go ahead and say it outright and stop beating around the bush like a petri-

fied fecking lummox. If you had seen anything made
you think I'd killed Oona deliberate, why so would
you've still come visiting me every night for the past
seven year?

MARY *finishes off her poteen with a flourish and puts the
glass down.*

MICK: Oh, just to cadge me fecking booze, was it? Well be off
on the road for yourself if that's the only reason you
come here, with your hour-long weather bulletins and
your Eamonn fecking Andrews spouting then. I never
laid a finger on Oona, not from the day we married to
the day she died, and if it's that you think you can upset
me saying you saw something that night when there
was nothing to see, then you've got another fecking
think coming, girlie.

MARY: I'm saying nothing. Nothing at all am I saying. All
I'm saying is you'll be meeting up with Oona again
someday, Mick Dowd, and not just the bare skull but the
spirit of her, and when you meet may down to the stinking fires of hell she drag the rotten murdering bones of
you, and may downhill from there for you it go. Goodbye to you now.

MARY *moves to the door.*

MICK: Maryjohnny?

MARY *turns.*

MICK: You've forgotten your fluorescent pens, there.

She picks the pens up.

MARY: Thank you.

MARY *goes to the door again.*

MICK: And Maryjohnny? *(Pause.)* I didn't touch her. I swear it.

> MARY *stares at him a moment, then exits.* MICK *looks at the rose locket then picks up the skull and stares at it a while, feeling the forehead crack. He rubs the skull against his cheek.*

MICK *(quietly)*: I swear it.

> *He caresses the skull again, then kisses the cranium gently. Lights slowly fade to black.*

The Lonesome West

The Lonesome West, a Druid Theatre Company/Royal Court Theatre co-production, was first presented at the Town Hall Theatre, Galway, on June 10, 1997, and subsequently opened at the Royal Court Theatre Downstairs on July 19, 1997. The cast was as follows:

GIRLEEN KELLEHER	Dawn Bradfield
FATHER WELSH	David Ganly
COLEMAN CONNOR	Maeliosa Stafford
VALENE CONNOR	Brian F. O'Byrne

Directed by Garry Hynes
Designed by Francis O'Connor
Lighting design by Ben Ormerod
Sound design by Bell Helicopter
Music by Paddy Cunneen

CHARACTERS

GIRLEEN KELLEHER, *seventeen, pretty.*
FATHER WELSH, *thirty-five.*
COLEMAN CONNOR
VALENE CONNOR

Setting: Leenane, a small town in Connemara, County Galway

SCENE ONE

The kitchen/living-room of an old farmhouse in Leenane, Galway. Front door far right, a table with two chairs down right, an old fireplace in the centre of the back wall, tattered armchairs to its right and left. Door to COLEMAN's room in the left back wall. Door to VALENE's room far left. A long row of dusty, plastic Catholic figurines, each marked with a black 'V', line a shelf on the back wall, above which hangs a double-barrelled shotgun and above that a large crucifix. A food cupboard on the wall left, a chest of drawers towards the right, upon which rests a framed photo of a black dog. As the play begins it is day. COLEMAN, dressed in black, having just attended a funeral, enters, undoing his tie. He takes a biscuit tin out of a cupboard, tears off the Sellotape that binds its lid and takes out from it a bottle of poteen, also marked with a 'V'. FATHER WELSH, a thirty-five-year-old priest, enters just behind him.

WELSH: I'll leave the door for Valene.

COLEMAN: Be doing what you like.

He pours two glasses as WELSH sits at the table.

You'll have a drink with me you will?

WELSH: I will, Coleman, so.

COLEMAN *(quietly)*: A dumb fecking question that was.

WELSH: Eh?

COLEMAN: I said a dumb fecking question that was.

WELSH: Why, now?

> COLEMAN *gives* WELSH *his drink without answering and sits at the table also.*

WELSH: Don't be swearing today of all days anyway, Coleman.

COLEMAN: I'll be swearing if I want to be swearing.

WELSH: After us only burying your dad, I'm saying.

COLEMAN: Oh aye, right enough, sure you know best, oh aye.

WELSH *(pause)*: Not a bad turnout anyways.

COLEMAN: A pack of vultures only coming nosing.

WELSH: Come on now, Coleman. They came to pay their last respects.

COLEMAN: Did seven of them, so, not come up asking where the booze-up after was to be held, and Maryjohnny then 'Will yet be having vol-au-vents?' There'll be no vol-au-vents had in this house for the likes of them. Not while Valene holds the purse-strings anyways. If it was me held the purse-strings I'd say aye, come around for yourselves, even if ye are vultures, but I don't hold the purse-strings. Valene holds the purse-strings.

WELSH: Valene does be a biteen tight with his money.

COLEMAN: A biteen? He'd steal the shite out of a burning pig, and this is his poteen too, so if he comes in shouting the odds tell him you asked me outright for it. Say you sure enough demanded. That won't be hard to believe.

WELSH: Like an alcoholic you paint me as half the time.

COLEMAN: Well that isn't a big job of painting. A bent child with no paint could paint you as an alcoholic. There's no great effort needed in that.

WELSH: I never touched the stuff before I came to this parish. This parish would drive you to drink.

COLEMAN: I suppose it would, only some people don't need as much of a drive as others. Some need only a short walk.

WELSH: I'm no alcoholic, Coleman. I like a drink is all.

COLEMAN: Oh aye, and I believe you too. *(Pause.)* Vol-au-vents, feck. The white-haired oul ghoulish fecking whore. She's owed me the price of a pint since nineteen-seventy-fecking-seven. It's always tomorrow with that bitch. I don't care if she does have Alzheimer's. If I had a vol-au-vent I'd shove it up her arse.

WELSH: That's not a nice thing to be saying about a . . .

COLEMAN: I don't care if it is or it isn't.

WELSH *(pause)*: This house, isn't it going to be awful lonesome now with yer dad gone?

COLEMAN: No.

WELSH: Ah it'll be a biteen lonesome I'm sure.

COLEMAN: If you're saying it'll be a biteen lonesome maybe it *will* be a biteen lonesome. I'll believe it if you're forcing it down me throat and sure aren't you the world's authority on lonesome?

WELSH: Are there no lasses on the horizon for ye, now ye're free and easy? Oh I'll bet there's hundreds.

COLEMAN: Only your mammy.

WELSH: It's a beautiful mood today you're in. *(Pause.)* Were you never in love with a girl, so, Coleman?

COLEMAN: I was in love with a girl one time, aye, not that it's any of your fecking business. At tech this was. Alison O'Hoolihan. This gorgeous red hair on her. But she got a pencil stuck in the back of her gob one day. She was sucking it the pointy-end inwards. She must've gotten a nudge. That was the end of me and Alison O'Hoolihan.

WELSH: Did she die, Coleman?

COLEMAN: She didn't die, no. I wish she had, the bitch. No, she got engaged to the bastarding doctor who wrenched the pencil out of her. Anybody could've done that job. It didn't need a doctor. I have no luck.

Pause. WELSH *drinks some more.* VALENE *enters with a carrier bag out of which he takes some new figurines and arranges them on the shelf.* COLEMAN *watches.*

VALENE: Fibreglass.

COLEMAN *(pause)*: Feck fibreglass.

VALENE: No, feck you instead of feck fibreglass.

COLEMAN: No, feck you two times instead of feck fibre-glass . . .

WELSH: Hey now!! (*Pause.*) Jesus!

VALENE: He started it.

WELSH (*pause*): Tom Hanlon I see he's back. I was speaking to him at the funeral. Did Tom know yer dad?

COLEMAN: Slightly he knew Dad. He arrested him five or six times for screaming at nuns.

WELSH: I remember hearing tell of that. That was an odd crime.

COLEMAN: Not that odd.

WELSH: Ah come on, now, it is.

COLEMAN: Oh if you say it is, Walsh, I suppose it is.

VALENE: I do hate them fecking Hanlons.

WELSH: Why now, Val?

VALENE: Why, is it? Didn't their Mairtin hack the ears off of poor Lassie, let him fecking bleed to death?

COLEMAN: You've no evidence at all it was Mairtin hacked the ears off of Lassie.

VALENE: Didn't he go bragging about it to Blind Billy Pender?

COLEMAN: That's only hearsay evidence. You wouldn't get that evidence to stand up in a court of law. Not from a blind boy anyways.

VALENE: I'd expect you to be agin me. Full well I'd expect it.

COLEMAN: That dog did nothing but bark anyways.

VALENE: Well barking doesn't deserve ears chopped off, Coleman. That's what dogs are supposed to do is bark, if you didn't know.

COLEMAN: Not at that rate of barking. They're meant to ease up now and then. That dog was going for the world's fecking barking record.

WELSH: And there's plenty enough hate in the world as it is, Valene Connor, without you adding to it over a dead dog.

VALENE: Nobody'll notice a biteen more hate, so, if there's plenty enough hate in the world.

WELSH: A nice attitude that is for a . . .

VALENE: Feck off and sling your sermons at Maureen Folan and Mick Dowd, so, if it's nice attitudes you're after, Walsh. Wouldn't that be more in your fecking line?

WELSH *bows his head and pours himself another drink.*

COLEMAN: That shut the fecker up.

VALENE: It did. You see how quick he is to . . . That's my fecking poteen now! What's the . . . eh?

COLEMAN: He did come in pegging orders for a drink, now. What was I supposed to say to him, him just sticking Dad in the ground for us?

VALENE: Your own you could've given him so.

COLEMAN: And wasn't I about to 'til I up and discovered me cupboard was bare.

VALENE: Bare again, was it?

COLEMAN: Bare as a bald fella's arse.

VALENE: Never unbare are your cupboards.

COLEMAN: I suppose they're not now, but isn't that life?

WELSH: And there's no such word as unbare.

   VALENE *stares at* WELSH *sternly.*

COLEMAN (*laughing*): He's right!

VALENE: Picking me up on me vocabulary is it, Walsh?

COLEMAN: It is, aye.

WELSH: I'm not now. I'm only codding ya, Val.

VALENE: And shaking the hands of Mick and Maureen weren't you, too, I saw you at the grave there, and passing chit-chat among ye . . .

WELSH: I was passing no chit-chat . . .

VALENE: A great parish it is you run, one of them murdered his missus, an axe through her head, the other her mammy, a poker took her brains out, and it's only chit-chatting it is you be with them? Oh aye.

WELSH: What can I do, sure, if the courts and the polis . . .

VALENE: Courts and the polis me arse. I heard the fella you represent was of a higher authority than the courts and the fecking polis.

WELSH (*sadly*): I heard the same thing, sure. I must've heard wrong. It seems like God has no jurisdiction in this town. No jurisdiction at all.

VALENE *takes his bottle, mumbling, and pours himself a drink. Pause.*

COLEMAN: That's a great word, I think.

VALENE: What word?

COLEMAN: Jurisdiction. I like J-words.

VALENE: Jurisdiction's too Yankee-sounding for me. They never stop saying it on *Hill Street Blues.*

COLEMAN: It's better than unbare anyways.

VALENE: Don't you be starting with me again, ya feck.

COLEMAN: I will do what I wish, Mr Figurine-man.

VALENE: Leave me figurines out of it.

COLEMAN: How many more do ya fecking need?

VALENE: Lots more! No, lots and lots more!

COLEMAN: Oh aye.

VALENE: And where's me felt-tip pen, too, so I'll be giving them me 'V'?

COLEMAN: I don't know where your fecking felt-tip pen is.

VALENE: Well you had it doing beards in me *Woman's Own* yesterday!

COLEMAN: Aye, and you wrenched it from me near tore me hand off.

VALENE: Is all you deserved . . .

COLEMAN: You probably went hiding it then.

On these words, VALENE *instantly remembers where his pen is and exits to his room. Pause.*

He's forever hiding things that fella.

WELSH: I'm a terrible priest, so I am. I can never be defending God when people go saying things agin him, and, sure, isn't that the main qualification for being a priest?

COLEMAN: Ah there be a lot worse priests than you, Father, I'm sure. The only thing with you is you're a bit too weedy and you're a terror for the drink and you have doubts about Catholicism. Apart from that you're a fine priest. Number one you don't go abusing poor gasurs, so, sure, doesn't that give you a head-start over half the priests in Ireland?

WELSH: That's no comfort at all, and them figures are over-exaggerated anyways. I'm a terrible priest, and I run a terrible parish, and that's the end of the matter. Two murderers I have on me books, and I can't get either of the beggars to confess it. About betting on the horses and impure thoughts is all them bastards ever confess.

COLEMAN: Em, only I don't think you should be telling me what people be confessing, Father. You can be excommunicated for that I think. I saw it in a film with Montgomery Clift.

WELSH: Do ya see? I'm shite sure.

COLEMAN: Too hard on yourself is all you are, and it's only pure gossip that Mick and Maureen murdered anybody, and nothing but gossip. Mick's missus was a pure drink-driving accident is unfortunate but could've happened to anybody . . .

WELSH: With the scythe hanging out of her forehead, now, Coleman?

COLEMAN: A pure drink-driving, and Maureen's mam only fell down a big hill and Maureen's mam was never steady on her feet.

WELSH: And was even less steady with the brains pouring out of her, a poker swipe.

COLEMAN: She had a bad hip and everybody knew, and if it's at anybody you should be pegging murder accusations, isn't it me? Shot me dad's head off him, point blank range.

WELSH: Aye, but an accident that was, and you had a witness . . .

COLEMAN: Is what I'm saying. And if Valene hadn't happened to be there to see my tripping and the gun falling, wouldn't the town be saying I put the barrel bang up agin him, blew the head off him on purpose? It's only because poor Mick and Maureen had no witnesses is why all them gobshites do go gossipping about them.

VALENE *returns with his pen and starts drawing 'V's on the new figurines.*

WELSH: See? You do see the good in people, Coleman. That's what I'm supposed to do, but I don't. I'm always at the head of the queue to be pegging the first stone.

VALENE: He's not having another fecking crisis of faith?

COLEMAN: He is.

VALENE: He never stops, this fella.

WELSH: Aye, because I have nothing to offer me parish at all.

COLEMAN: Sure haven't you just coached the under-twelves football to the Connaught semifinals yer first year trying?

WELSH: Ah the under-twelves football isn't enough to restore your faith in the priesthood, Coleman, and we're a bunch of foulers anyway.

COLEMAN: Ye aren't. Ye're skilful.

WELSH: Ten red cards in four games, Coleman. That's a world's record in girls' football. That'd be a record in boys' football. One of the lasses from St Angela's she's still in hospital after meeting us.

COLEMAN: If she wasn't up for the job she shouldn't've been on the field of play.

WELSH: Them poor lasses used to go off crying. Oh a great coach I am, oh aye.

COLEMAN: Sissy whining bitches is all them little feckers are.

A rap on the front door, then GIRLEEN, *a pretty girl of seventeen, puts her head round it.*

GIRLEEN: Are ye in need?

VALENE: Come in for yourself, Girleen. I'll be taking a couple of bottles off ya, aye. I'll get me money.

VALENE *exits to his room as* GIRLEEN *enters, taking two bottles of poteen out of her bag.*

GIRLEEN: Coleman. Father Welsh Walsh Welsh . . .

WELSH: Welsh.

GIRLEEN: Welsh. I know. Don't be picking me up. How is all?

COLEMAN: We've just stuck our dad in the ground.

GIRLEEN: Grand, grand. I met the postman on the road with a letter for Valene.

She lays an official-looking envelope on the table.

That postman fancies me, d'you know? I think he'd like to be getting into me knickers, in fact I'm sure of it.

COLEMAN: Him and the rest of Galway, Girleen.

WELSH *puts his head in his hands at this talk.*

GIRLEEN: Galway minimum. The EC more like. Well, a fella won't be getting into my knickers on a postman's wages. I'll tell you that, now.

COLEMAN: Are you charging for entry so, Girleen?

GIRLEEN: I'm tinkering with the idea, Coleman. Why, are you interested? It'll take more than a pint and a bag of Taytos, mind.

COLEMAN: I have a three-pound postal order somewhere I never used.

GIRLEEN: That's nearer the mark, now. *(To* WELSH*)*. What kind of wages do priests be on, Father?

WELSH: Will you stop now?! Will you stop?! Isn't it enough for a girl going round flogging poteen, not to go talking of whoring herself on top of it?!

GIRLEEN: Ah, we're only codding you, Father.

She fluffs her fingers through WELSH's *hair. He brushes her off.*

(To COLEMAN.*)* He's not having another crisis of faith is he? That's twelve this week. We should report him to Jesus.

WELSH *moans into his hands.* GIRLEEN *giggles slightly.* VALENE *enters and pays* GIRLEEN.

VALENE: Two bottles, Girleen.

GIRLEEN: Two bottles it is. You've a letter there.

COLEMAN: Buy me a bottle, Valene. I'll owe ya.

VALENE *(opening letter)*: Buy you a bottle me arse.

COLEMAN: Do ya see this fella?

GIRLEEN: You've diddled me out of a pound, Valene.

VALENE *pays up as if expecting it.*

VALENE: It was worth a go.

GIRLEEN: You're the king of stink-scum fecking filth-bastards you, ya bitch-feck, Valene.

WELSH: Don't be swearing like that now, Girleen . . .

GIRLEEN: Ah me hairy arse, Father.

VALENE *(re letter)*: Yes! It's here! It's here! Me cheque! And look how much too!

VALENE *holds the cheque up in front of* COLEMAN'S *face.*

COLEMAN: I see how much.

VALENE: Do ya see?

COLEMAN: I see now, and out of me face take it.

VALENE *(holding it closer)*: Do ya see how much, now?

181

COLEMAN: I see now.

VALENE: And all to me. Is it a closer look you do need?

COLEMAN: Out of me face take that thing now.

VALENE: But maybe it's closer you need to be looking now . . .

VALENE *rubs the cheque in* COLEMAN's *face.* COLEMAN *jumps up and grabs* VALENE *by the neck.* VALENE *grabs him in the same way.* GIRLEEN *laughs as they struggle together.* WELSH *darts drunkenly across and breaks the two apart.*

WELSH: Be stopping, now! What's the matter with ye?

WELSH *gets accidentally kicked as the brothers part. He winces.*

COLEMAN: I'm sorry, Father. I was aiming at that feck.

WELSH: Hurt that did! Bang on me fecking shin.

GIRLEEN: You'll know now how the lasses at St Angela's be feeling.

WELSH: What's the matter with ye at all, sure?

VALENE: He started it.

WELSH: Two brothers laying into each other the same day their father was buried! I've never heard the like.

GIRLEEN: It's all because you're such a terrible priest to them, Father.

WELSH *glares at her. She looks away, smiling.*

GIRLEEN: I'm only codding you, Father.

WELSH: What kind of a town is this at all? Brothers fighting and lasses peddling booze and two fecking murderers on the loose?

GIRLEEN: And me pregnant on top of it. *(Pause.)* I'm not really.

WELSH *looks at her and them sadly, moving somewhat drunkenly to the door.*

WELSH: Don't be fighting any more, now, ye's two. *(Exits.)*

GIRLEEN: Father Walsh Welsh has no sense of humour. I'll walk him the road home for himself, and see he doesn't get hit be a cow like the last time.

COLEMAN: See you so, Girleen.

VALENE: See you so, Girleen. (GIRLEEN *exits. Pause.*) That fella, eh?

COLEMAN *(in agreement)*: Eh? That fella.

VALENE: Jeez. Eh? If he found out you blew the head off Dad on purpose, he'd probably get three times as maudlin.

COLEMAN: He takes things too much to heart does that fella.

VALENE: Way too much to heart.

Blackout.

SCENE TWO

Evening. Against the back wall and blocking out the fire-place is now situated a large, new, orange stove with a big 'V' scrawled on its front. COLEMAN, *in glasses, sits in the armchair left, reading* Woman's Own, *a glass of poteen beside him.* VALENE *enters, carrying a bag. Slowly, deliberately, he places a hand on the stove in a number of places in case it's been used recently.* COLEMAN *snorts in disgust at him.*

VALENE: I'm checking.

COLEMAN: I can see you're checking.

VALENE: I like to have a little check with you around.

COLEMAN: That's what you do best is check.

VALENE: Just a biteen of a check, like. D'you know what I mean? In *my* opinion, like.

COLEMAN: I wouldn't touch your stove if you shoved a kettle up me arse.

VALENE: Is right, my stove.

COLEMAN: If you fecking paid me I wouldn't touch your stove.

VALENE: Well I won't be fecking paying you to touch me stove.

COLEMAN: I know well you won't, you tight-fisted feck.

VALENE: And *my* stove is right. Did *you* pay the three hundred? Did *you* get the gas fixed up? No. Who did? Me. My money. Was it your money? No, it was my money.

COLEMAN: I know well it was your money.

VALENE: If you'd made a contribution I'd've said go ahead and use me stove, but you didn't, so I won't.

COLEMAN: We don't even need a stove.

VALENE: You may not need a stove, but I need a stove.

COLEMAN: You never fecking eat, sure!

VALENE: I'll start! Aye, by Christ I'll start. *(Pause.)* This stove is mine, them figurines are mine, this gun, them chairs, that table's mine. What else? This floor, them cupboards, everything in this fecking house is mine, and you don't go touching, boy. Not without me express permission.

COLEMAN: It'll be hard not to touch your fecking floor, now.

VALENE: Not without me express . . .

COLEMAN: Unless I go fecking levitating.

VALENE: Not without me express . . .

COLEMAN: Like them darkies.

VALENE (*angrily*): Not without me express fecking permission I'm saying!

COLEMAN: Your express permission, oh aye.

VALENE: To *me* all this was left. To me and me alone.

COLEMAN: 'Twasn't left but 'twas *awarded*.

VALENE: Me and me alone.

COLEMAN: Awarded it was.

VALENE: And you don't go touching. (*Pause.*) What darkies?

COLEMAN: Eh?

VALENE: What darkies go levitating?

COLEMAN: Them darkies. On them carpets. Them levitating darkies.

VALENE: Them's Pakies. Not darkies at all!

COLEMAN: The same differ!

VALENE: Not at all the same differ! Them's Paki-men, same as whistle at the snakes.

COLEMAN: It seems like you're the expert on Paki-men!

VALENE: I *am* the expert on Paki-men!

COLEMAN: You probably go falling in love with Paki-men too, so! Oh I'm sure.

VALENE: Leave falling in love out of it.

COLEMAN: What did you get shopping, Mister 'I-want-to-marry-a-Paki-man'?

VALENE: What did I get shopping, is it?

VALENE *takes two figurines out of his bag and arranges them delicately on the shelf.*

COLEMAN: Ah for feck's sake . . .

VALENE: Don't be cursing now. Coleman. Not in front of the saints. Against God that is.

He takes eight packets of Taytos out of the bag and lays them on the table.

And some Taytos I got.

COLEMAN: Be getting McCoys if you're getting crisps.

VALENE: I'll be getting what I li—

COLEMAN: Ya fecking cheapskate.

VALENE *(pause. Glaring)*: I'm not getting some crisps taste exactly the same, cost double, Coleman.

COLEMAN: They don't taste the same and they have grooves.

VALENE: They do taste the same and feck grooves.

COLEMAN: Taytos are dried fecking filth and everybody knows they are.

VALENE: The crisp expert now I'm listening to. What matter if they're dried fecking filth? They're seventeen pee, and whose crisps are they anyways? They're my crisps.

COLEMAN: They're your crisps.

VALENE: My crisps and my crisps alone.

COLEMAN: Or get Ripples.

VALENE: Ripples me arse and I don't see you digging in your . . . what's this?

VALENE *picks up* COLEMAN's *glass and sniffs it.*

COLEMAN: What's wha?

VALENE: This.

COLEMAN: Me own.

VALENE: Your own my arse. You've no money to be getting your own.

COLEMAN: I do have.

VALENE: From where?

COLEMAN: Am I being interrogated now?

VALENE: You are.

COLEMAN: Feck ya so.

VALENE *takes his poteen out of his biscuit tin to check if any is missing.* COLEMAN *puts the magazine aside, takes his glasses off and sits at the table.*

VALENE: You've been at this.

COLEMAN: I haven't at all been at that.

VALENE: It seems very . . . reduced.

COLEMAN: Reduced me arse. I wouldn't be at yours if you shoved a fecking . . .

VALENE *(sipping it, uncertain)*: You've topped it up with water.

COLEMAN: Be believing what you wish. I never touched your poteen.

VALENE: Where would you get money for ... Me house insurance?! Oh you fecker ... !

VALENE desperately finds and examines his insurance book.

COLEMAN: I paid in your house insurance.

VALENE: This isn't Duffy's signature.

COLEMAN: It is Duffy's signature. Doesn't it say 'Duffy'?

VALENE: You paid it?

COLEMAN: Aye.

VALENE: Why?

COLEMAN: Oh to do you a favour, after all the favours you've done me over the years. Oh aye.

VALENE: It's easy enough to check.

COLEMAN: It *is* easy enough to check, and check ahead, ya feck. Check until you're blue in the face.

Confused, VALENE *puts the book away.*

It's not only money can buy you booze. No. Sex appeal it is too.

VALENE: Sex appeal? You? Your sex appeal wouldn't buy the phlegm off a dead frog.

COLEMAN: You have your own opinion and you're well entitled to it. Girleen's of the opposite opinion.

VALENE: Girleen? Me arse.

COLEMAN: Is true.

VALENE: Eh?

COLEMAN: I said let me have a bottle on tick and I'll be giving you a big kiss, now. She said 'If you let me be touching you below, sure you can have a bottle for nothing.' The deal was struck then and there.

VALENE: Girleen wouldn't touch you below if you bought her a pony, let alone giving poteen away on top of it.

COLEMAN: I can only be telling the God's honest truth, and how else would I be getting poteen for free?

VALENE (*unsure*): Me arse. (*Pause.*) Eh? (*Pause.*) Girleen's pretty. (*Pause.*) Girleen's awful pretty. (*Pause.*) Why would Girleen be touching you below?

COLEMAN: Mature men it is Girleen likes.

VALENE: I don't believe you at all.

COLEMAN: Don't so.

VALENE (*pause*): What did it feel like?

COLEMAN: What did what feel like?

VALENE: The touching below.

COLEMAN: Em, nice enough now.

VALENE (*unsure*): I don't believe you at all. (*Pause.*) No, I don't believe you at all.

COLEMAN *opens and starts eating a packet of* VALENE's *crisps.*

VALENE: Girleen wouldn't be touching you below. Never in the world would Girleen be touching y— (*Stunned.*) Who said you could go eating me crisps?!

COLEMAN: Nobody said.

VALENE: In front of me?!

COLEMAN: I decided of me own accord.

VALENE: You'll be paying me seventeen pee of your own accord so! And right now you'll be paying me!

COLEMAN: Right now, is it?

VALENE: It is!

COLEMAN: The money you have stashed?

VALENE: And if you don't pay up it's a batter I'll be giving you.

COLEMAN: A batter from you? I'd be as scared of a batter from a lemon.

VALENE: Seventeen pee I'm saying!

Pause. COLEMAN *slowly takes a coin out of his pocket and, without looking at it, slams it down on the table.* VA-LENE *looks at the coin.*

That's ten.

COLEMAN *looks at the coin, takes out another one and slams that down also.*

COLEMAN: You can keep the change.

VALENE: I can keep the change, can I?

He pockets the coins, takes out three pee, opens one of COLEMAN's *hands and places the money in it.*

I'm in no need of charity.

He turns away. Still sitting, COLEMAN *throws the coins hard at the back of* VALENE'S *head.*

Ya fecker ya!! Come on so!

COLEMAN *jumps up, knocking his chair over.*

COLEMAN: Come on so, is it?

VALENE: Pegging good money at me?!

COLEMAN: It is. And be picking that money up now, for your oul piggy-bank, ya little virgin fecking gayboy ya . . .

The two grapple, fall to the floor and roll around scuffling. WELSH *enters through the front door, slightly drunk.*

WELSH: Hey ye's two! Ye's two! (*Pause. Loudly.*) Ye's two!

COLEMAN (*irritated*): Wha?

WELSH: Tom Hanlon's just killed himself.

VALENE: Eh?

WELSH: Tom Hanlon's just killed himself.

VALENE (*pause*): Let go o' me neck, you.

COLEMAN: Let go o' me arm so.

The two slowly let go of each other and stand up, as WELSH *sits at the table, stunned.*

WELSH: He walked out into the lake from the oul jetty there. Aye, and kept walking. His body's on the shingle. His father had to haul me drunk out of Rory's to say a prayer o'er him, and me staggering.

VALENE: Tom Hanlon? Jeez. Sure I was only talking to Tom a day ago there. The funeral.

WELSH: A child seen him. Seen him sitting on the bench on the jetty, a pint with him, looking out across the lake to the mountains there. And when his pint was done he got up and started walking, the clothes still on him, and didn't stop walking. No. 'Til the poor head of him was under. And even then he didn't stop.

COLEMAN (*pause*): Ah I never liked that Tom fecking Hanlon. He was always full of himself, same as all fecking coppers . . .

WELSH (*angrily*): The poor man's not even cold yet, Coleman Connor. Do you have to be talking that way about him?

COLEMAN: I do, or if I'm not to be a hypocrite anyways I do.

VALENE: It's hypocrites now. Do you see this fella, Father? Ate a bag of me crisps just now without a by your leave . . .

COLEMAN: I paid you for them crisps . . .

VALENE: Then says he's not a hypocrite.

COLEMAN: I paid thruppence over the odds for them crisps, and how does eating crisps make you a hypocrite anyways?

VALENE: It just does. And interfering with a schoolgirl on top of it is another crime, Father.

COLEMAN: I interfered with no schoolgirl. I was interfered with *be* a schoolgirl.

VALENE: The same differ!

WELSH: What schoolgirl's this, now?

COLEMAN: Girleen this schoolgirl is. This afternoon there she came up and a fine oul time we had, oh aye.

WELSH: Girleen? Sure Girleen's been helping me wash the strips for the under-twelves football all day, never left me sight.

Embarrassed, COLEMAN *gets up and moves toward his room.* VALENE *blocks his way.*

VALENE: Aha! Aha! Now who's the virgin fecking gayboy, eh? Now who's the virgin fecking gayboy?

COLEMAN: Out of me way, now.

VALENE: *Now,* eh?

COLEMAN: Out of me way I'm saying.

VALENE: I knew well!

COLEMAN: Are you moving or am I moving ya?

VALENE: *Now* did I know well? Eh?

COLEMAN: Eh?

VALENE: Eh?

WELSH: Coleman, come back now. We . . .

COLEMAN: And you can shut your fecking gob too, Welsh or Walsh or whatever your fecking name is, ya priest! You don't go catching Coleman Connor out on lies and expect to be . . . and be expecting to . . . to be . . .

COLEMAN *enters his room, slamming its door.*

VALENE: You're a stuttering oul ass, so you are! 'To be . . . to be . . . to be . . .' *(To* WELSH.*)* Eh?

As VALENE *turns back to* WELSH, COLEMAN *dashes out, kicks the stove and dashes back to his room,* VALENE *trying and failing to catch him.*

Ya fecker, ya!

He checks the stove for damage.

Me good fecking stove! If there's any damage done to this stove it'll be you'll be paying for it, ya feck! Did you see that, Father? Isn't that man mad? *(Pause.)* Do ya like me new stove, Father? Isn't it a good one?

COLEMAN *(off)*: Do ya see that 'V' on his stove, Father? Do you think it's a V for Valene? It isn't. It's a V for Virgin, it is.

VALENE: Oh is it now . . . ?

COLEMAN *(off)*: V for virgin it is, uh-huh.

VALENE: When you're the king of the virgins?

COLEMAN *(off)*: Valene the Virgin that V stands for.

VALENE: The fecking king of them you are! And don't be listening at doors!

COLEMAN *(off)*: I'll be doing what I wish.

VALENE *checks stove again.* WELSH *is on the verge of tears.*

VALENE *(re stove)*: No, I think it's okay, now . . .

WELSH: You see, I come in to ye . . . and ye're fighting. Fair enough, now, that's all ye two ever do is fight. Ye'll never be changed. It's enough times I've tried . . .

VALENE: Are you crying, Father, or is it a bit of a cold you do have? Ah it's a cold . . .

WELSH: It's crying I am.

VALENE: Well I've never seen the like.

WELSH: 'Cos I come in, and I tell ya a fella's just gone and killed himself, a fella ye went to school with . . . a fella ye grew up with . . . a fella never had a bad word to say about anybody and did his best to be serving the community every day of his life . . . and I tell you he's killed himself be drowning, is a horrible way to die, and not only do ye not bat an eye . . . not only do ye not bat an eye but ye go arguing about crisps and stoves then!

VALENE: I batted an eye.

WELSH: I didn't notice that eye batted!

VALENE: I batted a big eye.

WELSH: Well I didn't notice it, now!

VALENE (*pause*): But isn't it a nice stove, Father?

WELSH *puts his head in his hands.* VALENE *goes to the stove.*

VALENE: Only a day I've had it fixed up. You can still smell as clean as it is. Coleman's forbid to touch it at all because Coleman didn't contribute a penny towards it, for Coleman doesn't *have* a penny to contribute towards it. (*Picks up the three pee.*) He has three pee, but three pee won't go too far towards a stove. Not too far at all. He threw this three pee at me head earlier, d'you know? (*In realisation, angrily.*) And if he has no money and he

wasn't interfered with, where the feck was it that poteen
did come from?! Coleman . . . !

WELSH *(screamed)*: Valene, you fecking fecker ya!!

VALENE: Wha? Oh, aye, poor Thomas.

VALENE *nods in phoney empathy.*

WELSH *(pause. Sadly, standing)*: I came up to get ye to come to
the lake with me, to be dragging poor Tom's body home
for himself. Will ye be helping now?

VALENE: I will be, Father. I will be.

WELSH *(pause)*: Feck. Two murders and a suicide now. Two
murders and a fecking suicide . . .

WELSH *exits, shaking his head.*

VALENE *(calling out)*: Sure, not your fault was it, Father. Don't
you be getting maudlin again! *(Pause.)* Coleman? I'm off
down . . .

COLEMAN *(off)*: I heard.

VALENE: Are ya coming so?

COLEMAN *(off)*: Not at all am I coming. To go humping a
dead policeman about the country? A dead policeman
used to laugh at me press-ups in PE? I don't fecking
think so, now.

VALENE: You forever bear a grudge, you. Ah anyways it's
good strong men Father Walsh does need helping him,
not virgin fecking gayboys couldn't pay a drunk monkey to go interfering with him.

VALENE *quickly exits.* COLEMAN *storms into the room to find him gone. He goes to the door and idles there, thinking, looking around the room. His gaze falls on the stove. He picks up some matches and opens the stove door.*

COLEMAN: A virgin fecking gayboy, is it? Shall we be having gas mark ten for no reason at all, now? We shall, d'you know?

He lights the stove, turns it up, closes its door and exits to his room. He returns a few seconds later and looks around the room.

For no reason at all, is it?

He takes a large oven-proof bowl out of a cupboard, places all of the figurines from the shelf into the bowl and puts the bowl inside the stove, closing its door afterwards.

Now we'll be seeing who's a virgin gayboy couldn't pay a monkey to interfere with him. I'll say we'll fecking see.

He pulls on his jacket, brushes his unkempt hair for two seconds with a manky comb, and exits through the front door. Blackout.

Scene Three

A few hours later. VALENE *and* WELSH *enter, slightly drunk.* VALENE *takes his poteen out of his tin and pours himself a glass.* WELSH *eyes it a little.*

VALENE: That was an awful business, eh?

WELSH: Terrible. Just terrible, now. And I couldn't say a thing to them. Not a thing.

VALENE: What could be said to them, sure? The only thing they wanted to hear was 'Your son isn't dead at all', and that wouldn't have worked. Not with him lying in their front room, dripping.

WELSH: Did you ever hear such crying, Valene?

VALENE: You could've filled a lake with the tears that family cried. Or a russaway at minimum.

WELSH (*pause*): A wha?

VALENE: A russaway. One of them russaways.

WELSH: Reservoir?

VALENE: Russaway, aye, and their Mairtin crying with the best of them. I've never seen Mairtin crying as hard. I suppose that's all you deserve for chopping the ears off a poor dog.

WELSH: I suppose if it's your only brother you lose you do cry hard.

VALENE: I wouldn't cry hard if I lost me only brother. I'd buy a big cake and have a crowd round.

WELSH: Ah Valene, now. If it's your own brother you can't get on with, how can we ever hope for peace in the world . . . ?

VALENE: Peace me arse and don't keep going on, you. You always do whine on this oul subject when you're drunk.

VALENE sits at the table with drink and bottle.

WELSH *(pause)*: A lonesome oul lake that is for a fella to go killing himself in. It makes me sad just to think of it. To think of poor Tom sitting alone there, alone with his thoughts, the cold lake in front of him, and him weighing up what's best, a life full of the loneliness that took him there but a life full of good points too. Every life has good points, even if it's only . . . seeing rivers, or going travelling, or watching football on the telly . . .

VALENE *(nodding)*: Football, aye . . .

WELSH: Or the hopes of being loved. And Thomas weighing all that up on the one hand, then weighing up a death in cold water on the other, and choosing the water. And first it strikes you as dumb, and a waste, 'You were thirty-eight years old, you had health and friends, there was plenty worse off fecks than you in the world, Tom Hanlon' . . .

VALENE: The girl born with no lips in Norway.

WELSH: I didn't hear about her.

VALENE: There was this girl in Norway, and she was born with no lips at all.

WELSH: Uh-huh. But then you say if the world's such a decent place worth staying in, where were his friends when he needed them in this decent world? When he needed them most, to say 'Come away from there, ya daft, we'd miss ya, you're worthwhile, as dumb as you are.' Where were his friends then? Where was I then? Sitting pissed on me own in a pub. (Pause.) Rotting in hell now, Tom Hanlon is. According to the Catholic Church anyways he is, the same as every suicide. No remorse. No mercy on him.

VALENE: Is that right now? Every suicide you're saying?

WELSH: According to us mob it's right anyways.

VALENE: Well I didn't know that. That's a turn-up for the books. (Pause.) So the fella from Alias Smith and Jones, he'd be in hell?

WELSH: I don't know the fella from Alias Smith and Jones.

VALENE: Not the blond one, now, the other one.

WELSH: I don't know the fella.

VALENE: He killed himself, and at the height of his fame.

WELSH: Well if he killed himself, aye, he'll be in hell too. (Pause.) It's great it is. You can kill a dozen fellas, you can kill two dozen fellas. So long as you're sorry after you can still get into heaven. But if it's yourself you go murdering, no. Straight to hell.

VALENE: That sounds awful harsh. (*Pause.*) So Tom'll be in hell now, he will? Jeez. (*Pause.*) I wonder if he's met the fella from *Alias Smith and Jones* yet? Ah, that fella must be old be now. Tom probably wouldn't even recognise him. That's if he saw *Alias Smith and Jones* at all. I only saw it in England. It mightn't've been on telly here at all.

WELSH (*sighing*): You wouldn't be sparing a drop of that poteen would ya, Valene? I've an awful thirst . . .

VALENE: Ah, Father, I have only a drop left and I need that for meself . . .

WELSH: You've half the bottle, sure . . .

VALENE: And if I had some I'd spare it, but I don't, and should priests be going drinking anyways? No they shouldn't, or anyways not on the night . . .

WELSH: Thou shouldst share and share alike the Bible says. Or somewhere it says . . .

VALENE: Not on the night you let one of your poor flock go murdering himself you shouldn't, is what me sentence was going to be.

WELSH: Well was that a nice thing to be saying?! Do I need that, now?!

VALENE (*mumbling*): Don't go trying to go cadging a poor fella's drink off him so, the wages you're on.

VALENE *gets up, puts the bottle back in his biscuit tin and carefully tapes the lid up, humming as he does so.*

WELSH: Is there a funny smell off of your house tonight, Val, now?

VALENE: If you're going criticising the smell of me house you can be off now, so you can.

WELSH: Like of plastic, now?

VALENE: Cadging me booze and then saying me house smells. That's the best yet, that is.

WELSH (*pause*): At least Coleman came down to help us with poor Thomas after all, even if he was late. But that was awful wrong of him to go asking Tom's poor mam if she'd be doing vol-au-vents after.

VALENE: That was awful near the mark.

WELSH: And her sitting there crying, and him nudging her then, and again and again 'Will ye be having vol-au-vents, Missus, will ye?'

VALENE: If he was drunk you could excuse it, but he wasn't. It was just out of spite. (*Laughing.*) Although it was funny, now.

WELSH: Where is he anyways? I thought he was walking the road with us.

VALENE: He'd stopped to do up his shoelaces a way back. (*Pause. In realisation.*) Coleman *has* no shoelaces. He has only loafers. (*Pause.*) Where have all me Virgin Marys gone?!

He leans in over the stove, placing his hands on its top, to see if the figurines have fallen down the back. The searing heat from the stove burns his hands and he pulls them away, yelping.

(Hysterical.) Wha?! Wha?!

WELSH: What is it, Valene? Did you go leaving your stove on?

Stunned, VALENE *opens the stove door with a towel. Smoke billows out. He takes the steaming bowl of molten plastic out, sickened, places it on the table and delicately picks up one of the half-melted figurines with the towel.*

All your figurines are melted, Valene.

VALENE *(staggering backwards)*: I'll kill the feck! I'll kill the feck!

WELSH: I'll be betting it was Coleman, Valene.

VALENE: That's all there is to it! I'll kill the feck!

VALENE *pulls the shotgun off the wall and marches around the room in a daze, as* WELSH *jumps up and tries to calm him.*

WELSH: Oh Valene now! Put that gun down!

VALENE: I'll blow the head off him! The fecking head off him I'll blow! I tell him not to touch me stove and I tell him not to touch me figurines and what does he do? He cooks me figurines in me stove! *(Looking into bowl.)* That one was blessed be the Pope! That one was given me mammy be Yanks! And they're all gone! All of them! They're all just the fecking heads and bobbing around!

WELSH: You can't go shooting you brother o'er inanimate objects, Valene! Give me that gun, now.

VALENE: Inanimate objects? Me figurines of the saints? And you call yoursel' a priest? No wonder you're the laughing stock of the Catholic Church in Ireland. And that takes some fecking doing, boy.

WELSH: Give it me now, I'm saying. Your own flesh and blood this is you're talking of murdering.

VALENE: Me own flesh and blood is right, and why not? If he's allowed to murder his own flesh and blood and get away with it, why shouldn't I be?

WELSH: What are you talking about, now? Coleman shooting your dad was a pure accident and you know well.

VALENE: A pure accident me arse! You're the only fecker in Leenane believes that shooting was an accident. Didn't Dad make a jibe about Coleman's hairstyle, and didn't Coleman dash out, pull him back be the hair and blow the poor skulleen out his head, the same as he'd been promising to do since the age of eight and Da trod on his Scalectrix, broke it in two . . .

COLEMAN *enters through the front door.*

COLEMAN: Well I did love that Scalectrix. It had glow in the dark headlamps.

VALENE *turns and points the gun at* COLEMAN. WELSH *backs off moaning, hands to his head.* COLEMAN *nonchalantly idles to the table and sits down.*

WELSH: It can't be true! It can't be true!

COLEMAN: Look at that fella gone pure white . . .

VALENE: No, shut up you! Don't be coming in mouthing after your fecking crimes . . .

WELSH: Tell me you didn't shoot your dad on purpose, Coleman. Please, now . . .

VALENE: This isn't about our fecking dad! This is about me fecking figurines!

COLEMAN: Do you see this fella's priorities?

VALENE: Melting figurines is against God outright!

WELSH: So is shooting your dad in the head, sure!

VALENE: And on gas mark ten!

WELSH: Tell me, Coleman, tell me, please. Tell me you didn't shoot your dad there on purpose. Oh tell me, now . . .

COLEMAN: Will you calm down, you? (Pause.) Of course I shot me dad on purpose.

WELSH starts groaning again.

COLEMAN: I don't take criticising from nobody. 'Me hair's like a drunken child's.' I'd only just combed me hair and there was nothing wrong with it! And I know well shooting your dad in the head is against God, but there's some insults that can never be excused.

VALENE: And cooking figurines is against God on top of it, if they're Virgin Mary figurines anyways.

COLEMAN: Is true enough, be the fella with the gun, and I'll tell you another thing that's against God, before this fella puts a bullet in me . . . (To WELSH.) Hey moany, are you listening . . . ?

WELSH: I'm listening, I'm listening, I'm listening . . .

COLEMAN: I'll tell you another thing that's against God. Sitting your brother in a chair, with his dad's brains dripping down him, and promising to tell everyone it was nothing but an accident . . .

VALENE: Shut up now, ya feck . . .

COLEMAN: So long as there and then you sign over everything your dad went and left you in his will . . .

WELSH: No . . . no . . . no . . .

COLEMAN: His house and his land and his tables and his chairs and his bit of money to go frittering away on shitey-arsed ovens you only got to torment me, ya feck . . .

WELSH: No, now . . . no . . .

VALENE: Be saying goodbye to the world, you, fecker!

COLEMAN: And fecking Taytos then, the worst crisps in the world . . .

VALENE *cocks the gun that's up against* COLEMAN'S *head.*

WELSH: No, Valene, no!

VALENE: I said say goodbye to the world, ya feck.

COLEMAN: Goodbye to the world, ya feck.

VALENE *pulls the trigger. There is a hollow click. He pulls the trigger again. Another click. A third time, and another click, as* COLEMAN *reaches in his pocket and takes out two shotgun cartridges.*

COLEMAN: Do you think I'm fecking stupid, now? *(To* WELSH.*)* Did you see that, Father? My own brother going shooting me in the head.

VALENE: Give me them fecking bullets, now.

COLEMAN: No.

VALENE: Give me them bullets I'm saying.

COLEMAN: I won't.

VALENE: Give me them fecking . . .

> VALENE *tries to wrench the bullets out of* COLEMAN's
> *clenched fist,* COLEMAN *laughing as he does so.* VALENE
> *grabs* COLEMAN *by the neck and they fall to the floor,*
> *grappling, rolling around the place.* WELSH *stares at the*
> *two of them dumbstruck, horrified. He catches sight of the*
> *bowl of steaming plastic beside him and, almost blankly,*
> *as the grappling continues, clenches his fists and slowly*
> *lowers them into the burning liquid, holding them under.*
> *Through clenched teeth and without breathing,* WELSH
> *manages to withhold his screaming for about ten or fifteen*
> *seconds until, still holding his fists under, he lets rip with*
> *a horrifying high-pitched wail lasting about ten seconds,*
> *during which* VALENE *and* COLEMAN *stop fighting,*
> *stand, and try to help him . . .*

VALENE: Father Walsh, now . . .

COLEMAN: Father Walsh, Father Walsh . . .

> WELSH *pulls his fists out of the bowl, red raw, stifles his*
> *screams again, looks over the shocked* VALENE *and* COLE-
> MAN *in despair and torment, smashes the bowl off the*
> *table and dashes out through the front door, his fists*
> *clutched to his chest in pain.*

WELSH *(exiting, screaming)*: Me name's *Welsh!!!*

> VALENE *and* COLEMAN *stare after him a moment or two.*

COLEMAN: Sure that fella's pure mad.

VALENE: He's outright mad.

COLEMAN: He's a lube. (*Gesturing at bowl.*) Will he be expecting us to clear his mess up?

VALENE *puts his head out the front door and calls out.*

VALENE: Will you be expecting us to clear your mess up, you?

COLEMAN (*pause*): What did he say?

VALENE: He was gone.

COLEMAN: A lube and nothing but a lube. (*Pause.*) Ah it's your fecking floor. You clean it up.

VALENE: You wha?!

COLEMAN: Do you see me nice bullets, Valene?

COLEMAN *rattles his two bullets in* VALENE'S *face, then exits to his room.*

VALENE: Ya fecking . . . !

COLEMAN'S *door slams shut.* VALENE *grimaces, pauses, scratches his balls blankly and sniffs his fingers. Pause. Blackout.*

Interval.

Scene Four

A plain bench on a lakeside jetty at night, on which
WELSH *sits with a pint, his hands lightly bandaged.*
GIRLEEN *comes over and sits down beside him.*

WELSH: Girleen.

GIRLEEN: Father. What are ya up to?

WELSH: Just sitting here, now.

GIRLEEN: Oh aye, aye. (*Pause.*) That was a nice sermon at Thomas's today, Father.

WELSH: I didn't see you there, did I?

GIRLEEN: I was at the back a ways. (*Pause.*) Almost made me go crying, them words did.

WELSH: You crying? I've never in all the years heard of you going crying, Girleen. Not at funerals, not at weddings. You didn't even cry when Holland knocked us out of the fecking World Cup.

GIRLEEN: Now and then on me own I go crying, over different things . . .

WELSH: That Pakie fecking Bonner. He couldn't save a shot from a fecking cow.

WELSH *sips his pint.*

GIRLEEN: I'd be saying you've had a few now, Father?

WELSH: Don't you be starting on me now. On top of everybody else.

GIRLEEN: I wasn't starting on ya.

WELSH: Not today of all days.

GIRLEEN: I wasn't starting at all on ya. I do tease you sometimes but that's all I do do.

WELSH: Sometimes, is it? All the time, more like, the same as everybody round here.

GIRLEEN: I do only tease you now and again, and only to camouflage the mad passion I have deep within me for ya . . .

WELSH *gives her a dirty look. She smiles.*

GIRLEEN: No, I'm only joking now, Father.

WELSH: Do ya see?!

GIRLEEN: Ah be taking a joke will ya, Father? It's only 'cos you're so high-horse and up yourself that you make such an easy target.

WELSH: I'm not so high-horse and up meself.

GIRLEEN: All right you're not so.

WELSH *(pause)*: *Am* I so high-horse and up meself?

GIRLEEN: No, now. Well, no more than most priests.

WELSH: Maybe I am high-horse so. Maybe that's why I don't fit into this town. Although I'd have to have killed half me fecking relatives to fit into this town. Jeez. I thought Leenane was a nice place when first I turned up here, but no. Turns out it's the murder capital of fecking Europe. Did *you* know Coleman had killed his dad on purpose?

GIRLEEN (*lowers head, embarrassed*): I think I did hear a rumour somewhere along the line . . .

WELSH: A fecking rumour? And you didn't bat an eye or go reporting it?

GIRLEEN: Sure I'm no fecking stool-pigeon and Coleman's dad was always a grumpy oul feck. He did kick me cat Eamonn there once.

WELSH: A fella deserves to die, so, for kicking a cat?

GIRLEEN (*shrugs*): It depends on the fella. And the cat. But there'd be a lot less cats kicked in Ireland, I'll tell ya, if the fella could rest-assured he'd be shot in the head after.

WELSH: You have no morals at all, it seems, Girleen.

GIRLEEN: I have plenty of morals only I don't keep whining on about them like some fellas.

WELSH (*pause*): Val and Coleman'll kill each other someday if somebody doesn't do something to stop them. It won't be me who stops them anyways. It'll be someone with guts for the job.

He takes out a letter and passes it to GIRLEEN.

I've written them a little lettereen here, Girleen, would you give it to them next time you see them?

GIRLEEN: Won't you be seeing them soon enough yourself?

WELSH: I won't be. I'm leaving Leenane tonight.

GIRLEEN: Leaving for where?

WELSH: Anywhere. Wherever they send me. Anywhere but here.

GIRLEEN: But why, Father?

WELSH: Ah lots of different reasons, now, but the three slaughterings and one suicide amongst me congregation didn't help.

GIRLEEN: But none of that was your fault, Father.

WELSH: Oh no?

GIRLEEN: And don't you have the under-twelves semifinal tomorrow morning to be coaching?

WELSH: Them bitches have never listened to me advice before. I don't see why they should go starting now. Nobody ever listens to my advice. Nobody ever listens to me at all.

GIRLEEN: I listen to you.

WELSH: (sarcastic): Ar that's great comfort.

GIRLEEN bows her head, hurt.

WELSH: And you don't listen to me either. How many times have I told you to stop flogging your dad's booze about town, and still you don't?

GIRLEEN: Ah it's just 'til I save up a few bob, Father, I'm doing that flogging.

WELSH: A few bob for what? To go skittering it away the clubs in Carraroe, and drunk schoolboys pawing at ya.

GIRLEEN: Not at all, Father. I do save it to buy a few nice things out me mam's Freeman's catalogue. They do have an array of . . .

WELSH: To go buying shite, aye. Well I wish I did have as tough problems in my life as you do in yours, Girleen. It does sound like life's a constant torment for ya.

GIRLEEN *stands up and wrenches* WELSH's *head back by the hair.*

GIRLEEN: If anybody else went talking to me that sarcastic I'd punch them in the fecking eye for them, only if I punched you in the fecking eye you'd probably go crying like a fecking girl!

WELSH: I never asked you to come sitting beside me.

GIRLEEN: Well I didn't know there was a law against sitting beside ya, although I wish there fecking was one now.

GIRLEEN *releases him and starts walking away.*

WELSH: I'm sorry for being sarcastic to you, Girleen, about your mam's catalogue and whatnot. I am.

GIRLEEN *stops, pauses, and idles back to the bench.*

GIRLEEN: It's okay.

WELSH: It's only that I'm feeling a bit . . . I don't know . . .

GIRLEEN *(sitting beside him)*: Maudlin.

WELSH: Maudlin. Maudlin is right.

GIRLEEN: Maudlin and lonesome. The maudlin and lonesome Father Walsh. *Welsh. (Pause.)* I'm sorry, Father.

WELSH: Nobody ever remembers.

GIRLEEN: It's just Walsh is so close to Welsh, Father.

WELSH: I know it is. I know it is.

GIRLEEN: What's your first name, Father?

WELSH *(pause)*: Roderick.

GIRLEEN *stifles laughter.* WELSH *smiles.*

GIRLEEN: Roderick? *(Pause.)* Roderick's a horrible name, Father.

WELSH: I know, and thanks for saying so, Girleen, but you're just trying to boost me spirits now, aren't ya?

GIRLEEN: I'm just being nice to ya now.

WELSH: What kind of a name's Girleen for a girl anyways? What's your proper first name?

GIRLEEN *(cringing)*: Mary.

WELSH *(laughing)*: Mary? And you go laughing at Roderick then?

GIRLEEN: Mary's the name of the mammy of Our Lord, did you ever hear tell of it?

WELSH: I heard of it somewhere along the line.

GIRLEEN: It's the reason she never got anywhere for herself. Fecking Mary.

WELSH: *You'll* be getting somewhere for yourself, Girleen.

GIRLEEN: D'ya think so, now?

WELSH: As tough a get as you are? Going threatening to thump priests? Of course.

GIRLEEN *brushes the hair out of* WELSH's *eyes.*

GIRLEEN: I wouldn't have gone thumping you, now, Father.

She gently slaps his cheek.

Maybe a decent slapeen, now.

WELSH *smiles and faces front.* GIRLEEN *looks at him, then away, embarrassed.*

WELSH *(pause)*: No, I just came out to have a think about Thomas before I go on me way. Say a little prayer for him.

GIRLEEN: It's tonight you're going?

WELSH: It's tonight, aye. I said to meself I'll stay for Tom's funeral, then that'll be the end of it.

GIRLEEN: But that's awful quick. No one'll have a chance to wish you goodbye, Father.

WELSH: Goodbye, aye, and good riddance to the back of me.

GIRLEEN: Not at all.

WELSH: No?

GIRLEEN: No.

Pause. WELSH *nods, unconvinced, and drinks again.*

Will you write to me from where you're going and be giving me your new address, Father?

WELSH: I'll try, Girleen, aye.

GIRLEEN: Just so's we can say hello now and then, now.

WELSH: Aye, I'll try.

As he speaks, GIRLEEN *manages to stifle tears without him noticing.*

This is where he walked in from, d'you know? Poor Tom. Look at as cold and bleak as it is. Do you think it took courage or stupidity for him to walk in, Girleen?

GIRLEEN: Courage.

WELSH: The same as that.

GIRLEEN: And Guinness.

WELSH *(laughing)*: The same as that. *(Pause.)* Look at as sad and as quiet and still.

GIRLEEN: It's more than Thomas has killed himself here down the years, d'you know, Father? Three other fellas walked in here, me mam was telling me.

WELSH: Is that right now?

GIRLEEN: Years and years ago this is. Maybe even famine times.

WELSH: Drowned themselves?

GIRLEEN: This is where they all come.

WELSH: We should be scared of their ghosts so but we're not scared. Why's that?

GIRLEEN: You're not scared because you're pissed to the gills. I'm not scared because . . . I don't know why. One, because you're here, and two, because . . . I don't know. I don't be scared of cemeteries at night either. The opposite of that, I do *like* cemeteries at night.

WELSH: Why, now? Because you're a morbid oul tough?

GIRLEEN *(embarrassed throughout)*: Not at all. I'm not a tough. It's because . . . even if you're sad or something, or lonely or something, you're still better off than them lost in the ground or in the lake, because . . . at least you've got the *chance* of being happy, and even if it's a real little chance, it's more than them dead ones have. And it's not that you're saying 'Hah, I'm better than ye', no, because in the long run it might end up that you have a worse life than ever they had and you'd've been better off as dead as them, there and then. But at least when you're still here there's the *possibility* of happiness, and it's like them dead ones know that, and they're happy for you to have it. They say 'Good luck to ya.' *(Quietly.)* Is the way I see it anyways.

WELSH: You have a million thoughts going on at the back of them big brown eyes of yours.

GIRLEEN: I never knew you did ever notice me big brown eyes. Aren't they gorgeous, now?

WELSH: You'll grow up to be a mighty fine woman one day, Girleen, God bless you.

WELSH *drinks again.*

GIRLEEN *(quietly, sadly)*: One day, aye. *(Pause.)* I'll be carrying on the road home for meself now, Father. Will you be staying or will you be walking with me?

WELSH: I'll be staying a biteen longer for meself, Girleen. I'll be saying that prayer for poor Thomas, now.

GIRLEEN: It's goodbye for a while so.

WELSH: It is.

GIRLEEN *kisses his cheek and they hug.* GIRLEEN *stands.*

WELSH: You'll remember to be giving that letter to Valene and Coleman, now, Girleen?

GIRLEEN: I will. What's in it, Father? It does sound very mysterious. It wouldn't be packed full of condoms for them, would it?

WELSH: It wouldn't at all, now!

GIRLEEN: 'Cos, you know, Valene and Coleman'd get no use out of them, unless they went using them on a hen.

WELSH: Girleen, now . . .

GIRLEEN: And it'd need to be a blind hen.

WELSH: You do have a terrible mouth on ya.

GIRLEEN: Aye, all the better to . . . no, I won't be finishing that sentence. Did you hear tell of Valene's new hobby, Father? He's been roaming the entirety of Connemara picking up new figurines of the saints for himself, but only ceramic and china ones won't go melting away on him. Thirty-seven of them at last count he has, and only to go tormenting poor Coleman.

WELSH: Them two, they're just odd.

GIRLEEN: They *are* odd. They're the kings of odd. (*Pause.*) See you so, Father.

WELSH: See you so, Girleen. Or Mary, is it?

GIRLEEN: If you let me know where you get to I'll write with how the under-twelves get on tomorrow. It may be in the *Tribune* anyways. Under 'Girl decapitated in football match'.

WELSH *nods, half smiles.* GIRLEEN *idles away.*

WELSH: Girleen, now? Thanks for coming sitting next to me. It's meant something to me, it has.

GIRLEEN: Any time, Father. Any time.

GIRLEEN *exits.* WELSH *stares out front again.*

WELSH (*quietly*): No, not any time, Girleen. Not any time.

WELSH *finishes his pint, puts the glass down, blesses himself and sits there quietly a moment, thinking. Blackout.*

SCENE FIVE

Stage in darkness apart from WELSH, *who recites his letter rapidly.*

WELSH: Dear Valene and Coleman, it is Father Welsh here. I am leaving Leenane for good tonight and I wanted to be saying a few words to you, but I won't be preaching at you for why would I be? It has never worked in the past and it won't work now. All I want to do is be pleading with you as a fella concerned about ye and yer lives, both in this world and the next, and the next won't be too long away for ye's if ye keep going on as mad as ye fecking have been. Coleman, I will not be speaking here about your murdering of your dad, although obviously it does concern me, both as a priest and as a person with even the vaguest moral sense, but that is a matter for your own conscience, although I hope some day you will realise what you have done and go seeking forgiveness for it, because let me tell you this, getting your hairstyle insulted is no just cause to go murdering someone, in fact it's the worst cause I did ever hear. But I will leave

it at that although the same goes for you, Valene, for
your part in your dad's murdering, and don't go saying
you had no part because you did have a part and a big
part. Going lying that it was an accident just to get your
father's money is just as dark a deed as Coleman's deed,
if not more dark, for Coleman's deed was done out of
temper and spite, whereas your deed was done out of
being nothing but a money-grubbing fecking miser with
no heart at all, but I said I would not be preaching at
you and I have lost me thread anyways so I will stop
preaching at you and be starting a new paragraph.
(Pause.) Like I said, I am leaving tonight, but I have been
thinking about ye non-stop since the night I did scald
me hands there at yeres. Every time the pain does go
through them hands I do think about ye, and let me tell
you this. I would take that pain and pain a thousand
times worse, and bear it with a smile, if only I could restore to ye the love for each other as brothers ye do so
woefully lack, that must have been there some day.
Didn't as gasurs ye love each other? Or as young men,
now? Where did it all go on ye? Don't ye ever think
about it? What I think I think what ye've done is bury
it deep down in ye, under a rack of grudges and hate
and sniping like a pair of fecking oul women. Ye two
are like a pair of fecking oul women, so ye are, arguing
over fecking Taytos and stoves and figurines, is an arse-
brained argument. But I do think that yere love is still
there under all of that, in fact I'd go betting everything
that's dear to me on it, and may I rot in hell for ever if
I'm wrong. All it is is ye've lived in each other's pockets
the entire of yere lives, and a sad and lonesome exis-
tence it has been, with no women to enter the picture for

either of ye to calm ye down, or anyways not many women or the wrong sort of women, and what's happened the bitterness has gone building up and building up without check, the daily grudges and faults and moans and baby-crimes against each other ye can never seem to step back from and see the love there underneath and forgive each other for. Now, what the point of me letter is, couldn't ye do something about it? Couldn't the both of ye, now, go stepping back and be making a listeen of all the things about the other that do get on yere nerves, and the wrongs the other has done all down through the years that you still hold against him, and be reading them lists out, and be discussing them openly, and be taking a deep breath then and be forgiving each other them wrongs, no matter what they may be? Would that be so awful hard, now? It would for ye two, I know, but couldn't ye just be trying it, now? And if it doesn't work it doesn't work, but at least ye could say ye'd tried and would ye be any worse off? And if ye wouldn't be doing it for yourselves, wouldn't ye be doing it for me, now? For a friend of yeres, who cares about ye, who doesn't want to see ye blowing the brains out of each other, who never achieved anything as a priest in Leenane, in fact the opposite, and who'd see ye two becoming true brothers again as the greatest achievement of his whole time here. Sure it would be bordering on the miraculous. I might be canonised after. *(Pause.)* Valene and Coleman, I'm betting everything on ye. I know for sure there's love there somewheres, it's just a case of ye stepping back and looking for it. I'd be willing to bet me own soul that that love is there, and I know well the odds are stacked against me. They're probably

64,000 to one be this time, but I'd go betting on ye's still,
for despite everything, despite yere murder and yere
mayhem and yere miserliness that'd tear the teeth out o:
broken goats, I have faith in ye. You wouldn't be letting
me down now, would ye? Yours sincerely, and your
with the love of Christ now, Roderick Welsh.

Pause. WELSH *shivers slightly. Blackout.*

Scene Six

VALENE's *house. Shotgun back on wall, over shelf full of new ceramic figurines, all marked with a 'V'.* COLEMAN, *in glasses, sits in the armchair left, glass of poteen beside him, perusing another women's magazine.* VALENE *enters carrying a bag and places his hand on the stove in a number of places. Irritated,* COLEMAN *tries to ignore him.*

VALENE: I'm checking. (*Pause.*) It's good to have a little check. (*Pause.*) I think it is, d'you know? (*Pause.*) Just a *little* check. D'you know what I mean, like?

After a while more of this, VALENE *takes some new ceramic figurines out of his bag, which he arranges with the others on the shelf.*

COLEMAN: Ah for . . .

VALENE: Eh?

COLEMAN: Eh?

VALENE: Now then, eh?

COLEMAN: Uh-huh?

VALENE: Eh? Nice, I think. Eh? What do *you* think, Coleman?

COLEMAN: I think you can go feck yourself.

VALENE: No, not feck meself at all, now. Or over to the left a biteen would they look better? Hmm, we'll put the new St Martin over here, so it balances out with the other St Martin over there, so's we have one darkie saint on either side, so it balances out symmetrical, like. *(Pause.)* I'm a great one for shelf arranging I am. It is a skill I did never know I had. *(Pause.)* Forty-six figurines now. I'm sure to be getting into heaven with this many figurines in me house.

VALENE *finds his pen and marks up the new figurines.*

COLEMAN *(pause)*: There's a poor girl born in Norway here with no lips.

VALENE *(pause)*: That's old news that lip girl is.

COLEMAN: That girl'll never be getting kissed. Not with the bare gums on her flapping.

VALENE: She's the exact same as you, so, if she'll never be getting kissed, and you've no excuse. You've the full complement of lips.

COLEMAN: I suppose a million girls you've kissed in your time. Oh aye.

VALENE: Nearer two million.

COLEMAN: Two million, aye. And all of them aunties when you was twelve.

VALENE: Not aunties at all. Proper women.

COLEMAN: Me brother Valentine does be living in his own little dream-world, with the sparrows and the fairies and the hairy little men. Puw-ooh! And the daisy people.

VALENE (*pause*): I hope that's not my poteen.

COLEMAN: It's not at all your poteen.

VALENE: Uh-huh? (*Pause.*) Did you hear the news?

COLEMAN: I did. Isn't it awful?

VALENE: It's a disgrace. It's an outright disgrace, and nothing but. You can't go sending off an entire girl's football team, sure.

COLEMAN: Not in a semi-fecking-final anyways.

VALENE: Not at any time, sure. If you have to send people off you send them off one at a time, for their individual offences. You don't go slinging the lot of them off wholesale, and only seven minutes in, so they go crying home to their mammys.

COLEMAN: St Josephine's have only got through be default, and nothing but default. If they had any honour they'd not take their place in the final at all and be giving it to us.

VALENE: I hope they lose the final.

COLEMAN: The same as that, *I* hope they lose the final. Sure, with their goalie in a coma they're bound to.

VALENE: No, their goalie came out of her coma a while ago there. Intensive care is all she's in now.

COLEMAN: She was fecking feigning? Getting us expelled from all competitions for no reason at all? I hope she relapses into her coma and dies.

VALENE: The same as that, *I* hope she lapses into her coma and dies. (*Pause.*) Look at us, we're in agreement.

COLEMAN: We are, I suppose.

VALENE: We can agree sometimes.

He snatches the magazine out of COLEMAN's *hands.*

Except don't go reading me magazines, I've told you, 'til I've finished reading them.

He sits at the table and flips through the magazine without reading it. COLEMAN *fumes.*

COLEMAN (*standing*): And don't go . . . don't go tearing them out of me fecking hands, near tore the fingers off me!

VALENE: Have these fingers you (*V-sign.*) and take them to bed with ya.

COLEMAN: You're not even reading that *Take a Break.*

VALENE: I *am* reading this *Take a Break,* or anyways I'm glancing through this *Take a Break* at me own pace, as a fella's free to do if it's with his own money he goes buying his *Take a Break.*

COLEMAN: Only women's magazines is all you ever go reading. Sure without doubt it's a fecking gayboy you must be.

VALENE: There's a lad here in Bosnia and not only has he no arms but his mammy's just died. (*Mumbles as he reads, then*) Ah they're only after fecking money, the same as ever.

COLEMAN: And no fear of you sending that poor no-armed boy any money, ah no.

VALENE: They've probably only got him to put his arms behind his back, just to cod ya.

COLEMAN: It's any excuse for you.

VALENE: And I bet his mammy's fine.

COLEMAN (*pause*): Get *Bella* if you're getting magazines. *Take a Break*'s nothing but quizzes.

VALENE: There's a coupon here for Honey Nut Loops.

VALENE *starts carefully tearing out the coupon at the same time as* COLEMAN *quietly takes some Taytos out of a cupboard.*

COLEMAN: Quizzes and deformed orphans. (*Pause.*) Em, would you let me be having a bag of Taytos, Val? I'm hungry a biteen.

VALENE (*looking up. Pause*): Are you being serious, now?

COLEMAN: G'wan. I'll owe you for them.

VALENE: Put that bag back, now.

COLEMAN: I'll owe you for them, I'm saying. You can put them on the same bill you've put your melted figurines.

VALENE: Put them ... put them ... What are you doing, now? Put them Taytos back, I said.

COLEMAN: Valene, listen to me . . .

VALENE: No . . .

COLEMAN: I'm hungry and I need some Taytos. Didn't I wait 'til you came back in to ask you, now, and only because I'm honest . . .

VALENE: And you've asked me and I've said no. Slinging insults at me Taytos the other week I remember is all you were. I see the boot's on the other foot now.

COLEMAN: I've asked polite, now, Valene, and feck boots. Three times I've asked polite.

VALENE: I know well you've asked polite, Coleman. You've asked awful polite. And what I'm saying to ya, ya can't have any of me fecking Taytos, now!

COLEMAN: Is that your final word on the subject?

VALENE: It *is* me final word on the subject.

COLEMAN *(pause)*: I won't have any of your Taytos so. *(Pause.)* I'll just crush them to skitter.

He crushes the crisps to pulp and tosses the packet at VA-LENE. VALENE darts up and around the table to get at COLEMAN, during which time COLEMAN grabs two more packets from the cupboard and holds them up, one in each hand, threatening to crush them also.

Back off!

VALENE *stops dead in his tracks.*

COLEMAN: Bake off or they'll be getting the same!

VALENE *(scared)*: Be leaving me crisps now, Coleman.

COLEMAN: Be leaving them, is it? When all I wanted was to go buying one of them and would've paid the full whack, but oh no.

VALENE (*tearfully, choking*): That's a waste of good food that is, Coleman.

COLEMAN: Good food, is it?

VALENE: There's Bosnians'd be happy to have them Taytos.

COLEMAN opens one of the bags and starts eating just as the front door bangs open and GIRLEEN *enters, face blotchy, letter in hand.*

COLEMAN: They *are* good food, d'you know?

GIRLEEN (*in shock throughout*): Have ye heard the news, now?

COLEMAN: What news, Girleen? The under-twelves . . . ?

Seeing COLEMAN *distracted,* VALENE *dives for his neck, trying to get the crisps off him at the same time. They drag each other to the floor, rolling and scuffling,* COLEMAN *purposely mashing up the crisps any chance he gets.* GIRLEEN *stares at them a while, then quietly takes a butcher's knife out of one of the drawers, goes over to them, pulls* COLEMAN's *head back by the hair and puts the knife to his neck.*

VALENE: Leave Coleman alone, Girleen. What are you doing, now?

GIRLEEN: I'm breaking ye up.

COLEMAN (*scared*): We're broke up.

VALENE (*scared*): We're broke up.

Once the two are separated, GIRLEEN *lets* COLEMAN *go and puts the letter on the table, sadly.*

GIRLEEN: There's a letter there Father Welsh wrote ye.

VALENE: What does that feck want writing to us?

COLEMAN: Going moaning again, I'll bet.

VALENE picks the letter up, COLEMAN *pulls it off him,* VALENE *pulls it back. They stand reading it together,* COLEMAN *getting bored after a few seconds.* GIRLEEN *takes out a heart pendant on a chain and looks at it.*

GIRLEEN: I read it already on ye, coming over. All about the two of ye loving each other as brothers it is.

COLEMAN *(stifling laughter)*: Wha?

VALENE: Father Walsh Welsh's leaving, it looks like.

COLEMAN: Is it full of moaning, Valene? It is.

VALENE: And nothing but moaning. *(Mimicking.)* 'Getting your hairstyle insulted is no just cause to go murdering someone, in fact it's the worst cause I did ever hear.'

COLEMAN *(laughing)*: That was a funny voice.

GIRLEEN: I did order him this heart on a chain out of me mam's Freeman's catalogue. Only this morning it came. I asked him to be writing me with his new address last night, so I could send it on to him. I'd've never've got up the courage to be giving it him to his face. I'd've blushed the heart out of me. Four months I've been saving up to buy it him. All me poteen money. *(Crying.)* All me poteen money gone. I should've skittered it away the boys in Carraroe, and not go pinning me hopes on a feck I knew full well I'd never have.

GIRLEEN *cuts the chain in two with the knife.*

COLEMAN: Don't be cutting your good chain there, Girleen.

VALENE: Be leaving your chaineen there now, Girleen. That chain looks worth something.

GIRLEEN *tosses the chain in a corner.*

GIRLEEN *(sniffling)*: Have you read the letter there, now?

VALENE: I have. A pile of oul bull.

GIRLEEN: I read it to see if he mentioned me. Not a word.

COLEMAN: Just shite is it, Valene? It's not worth reading?

VALENE: Not at all.

COLEMAN: I'll leave it so, for I've no time for letters. I've never seen the sense in them. They're just writing.

GIRLEEN: I did like the bit about him betting his soul on ye. Didn't ye like that bit?

VALENE *picks up the broken chain.*

VALENE: I don't think I understood that bit.

GIRLEEN *(pause)*: Father Welsh drowned himself in the lake last night, same place as Tom Hanlon. They dragged his body out this morning. His soul in hell he's talking about, that only ye can save for him. *(Pause.)* You notice he never asked me to go saving his soul. I'd've liked to've saved his soul. I'd've been honoured, but no. *(Crying.)* Only mad drunken pig-shite feck-brained thicks he goes asking.

Shocked, COLEMAN *reads the letter.* GIRLEEN *goes to the door.* VALENE *offers the pendant out to her.*

VALENE: Your heart, Girleen, be keeping it for yourself.

GIRLEEN *(crying)*: Feck me heart. Feck it to hell. Toss it into fecking skitter's the best place for that fecking heart. *(Exiting.)* Not even a word to me!

After GIRLEEN *exits,* VALENE *sits in an armchair, looking at the chain.* COLEMAN *finishes reading the letter, leaves it on the table and sits in the opposite armchair.*

VALENE: Did you read it?

COLEMAN: I did.

VALENE *(pause)*: Isn't it sad about him?

COLEMAN: It *is* sad. Very sad.

VALENE *(pause)*: Will we be trying for ourselves? To get along, now?

COLEMAN: We will.

VALENE: There's no harm in trying.

COLEMAN: No harm at all, sure.

VALENE *(pause)*: Poor Father Welsh Walsh Welsh.

COLEMAN: Welsh.

VALENE: Welsh. *(Pause.)* I wonder why he did it?

COLEMAN: I suppose he must've been upset o'er something.

VALENE: I suppose. *(Pause.)* This is a pricey chain. *(Pause.)* We'll be giving it back to her next time we see her. She's only shocked now.

COLEMAN: Aye. She's not in her right mind at all. She did hurt me hair when she tugged at it too, d'you know?

VALENE: It did look like it hurt.

COLEMAN: It did hurt.

VALENE: *(pause)*: Father Welsh going topping himself does put arguing o'er Taytos into perspective anyways.

COLEMAN: It does.

VALENE: Eh?

COLEMAN: It does.

VALENE: Aye. Awful perspective. Awful perspective.

COLEMAN *(pause)*: Did you see 'Roderick' his name is?

VALENE *(snorts)*: I did.

COLEMAN *(pause. Seriously)*: We shouldn't laugh.

VALENE *nods. Both pull serious faces. Blackout.*

Scene Seven

Room tidier. WELSH's letter pinned to the foot of the cru-
cifix. VALENE and COLEMAN enter dressed in black, hav-
ing just attended WELSH's funeral, COLEMAN carrying a
small plastic bag full of sausage rolls and vol-au-vents.
He sits at the table. VALENE opens his poteen biscuit tin.

VALENE: That's that, then.

COLEMAN: That's that, aye. That's Father Welsh gone.

VALENE: A good do.

COLEMAN: Aye. It's often a good do when it's a priest they're
sticking away.

COLEMAN empties his bag onto table.

VALENE: You didn't have to go nabbing a whole bagful, now,
Coleman.

COLEMAN: Didn't they offer, sure?

VALENE: But a whole bagful, I'm saying.

COLEMAN: It'd have only gone to waste, and sure a bagful won't be going very far between us.

VALENE: Between us?

COLEMAN: Of course between us.

VALENE: Ohh.

They both eat a little.

These are nice vol-au-vents.

COLEMAN: They *are* nice vol-au-vents.

VALENE: You can't say the Catholic Church doesn't know how to make a nice vol-au-vent, now.

COLEMAN: It's their best feature. And their sausage rolls aren't bad either, although they probably only buy them in.

VALENE *(pause)*: Em, would you be having a glass of poteen with me, Coleman?

COLEMAN *(shocked)*: I would, now. If you can spare a drop, like.

VALENE: I can easy spare a drop.

VALENE pours two glasses, one bigger than the other, thinks about it, then gives COLEMAN *the bigger.*

COLEMAN: Thank you, Valene. Sure we have our own little feasteen now.

VALENE: We do.

COLEMAN: D'you remember when as gasurs we did used to put the blankets o'er the gap between our beds and hide under them like a tent it was o'er us, and go having a feasteen of oul jammy sandwiches then?

VALENE: That was you and Mick Dowd used to go camping in the gap between our beds. You'd never let me be in with yous at all. Ye used to step on me head if I tried to climb into that camp with you. I still remember it.

COLEMAN: Mick Dowd, was it? I don't remember that at all, now. I did think it was you.

VALENE: Half me childhood you spent stepping on me head, and for no reason. And d'you remember when you pinned me down and sat across me on me birthday and let the stringy spit dribble out your gob and let down and down it dribble 'til it landed in me eye then?

COLEMAN: I remember it well, Valene, and I'll tell you this. I did mean to suck that spit back up just before it got to your eye, but what happened I lost control o'er it.

VALENE: And on me birthday.

COLEMAN (*pause*): I do apologise for dribbling in your eye and I do apologise for stepping on your head, Valene. On Father Welsh's soul I apologise.

VALENE: I do accept your apology so.

COLEMAN: Although plenty of times as a gasur I remember you dropping stones on me head while I was asleep and big stones.

VALENE: Only in retaliation them stones ever was.

COLEMAN: Retaliation or not. Waking up to stones dropped on ya is awful frightening for a small child. And retaliation doesn't count anyways if it's a week later. It's only then and there retaliation does apply.

VALENE: I do apologise for dropping stones on you so. *(Pause.)* For your brain never did recover from them injuries, did it, Coleman?

COLEMAN *stares at* VALENE *a second, then smiles.* VALENE *smiles also.*

VALENE: This is a great oul game, this is, apologising. Father Welsh wasn't too far wrong.

COLEMAN: I hope Father Welsh isn't in hell at all. I hope he's in heaven.

VALENE: *I* hope he's in heaven.

COLEMAN: Or purgatory at worst.

VALENE: Although if he's in hell at least he'll have Tom Hanlon to speak to.

COLEMAN: So it won't be as if he doesn't know anybody.

VALENE: Aye. And the fella off *Alias Smith and Jones.*

COLEMAN: Is the fella off *Alias Smith and Jones* in hell?

VALENE: He is. Father Welsh was telling me.

COLEMAN: The blond one.

VALENE: No, the other one.

COLEMAN: He was good, the other one.

VALENE: He was the best one.

COLEMAN: It's always the best ones go to hell. Me, probably straight to heaven I'll go, even though I blew the head off poor Dad. So long as I go confessing to it anyways. That's the good thing about being Catholic. You can shoot your dad in the head and it doesn't even matter at all.

VALENE: Well it matters a little bit.

COLEMAN: It matters a little bit but not a big bit.

VALENE *(pause)*: Did you see Girleen crying her eyes out, the funeral?

COLEMAN: I did.

VALENE: Poor Girleen. And her mam two times has had to drag her screaming from the lake at night, did you hear, there where Father Walsh jumped, and her just standing there, staring.

COLEMAN: She must've like Father Welsh or something.

VALENE: I suppose she must've. *(Taking out GIRLEEN's chain.)* She wouldn't take her chaineen back at all. She wouldn't hear tell of it. I'll put it up here with his letter to us.

He attaches the chain to the cross, so the heart rests on the letter, which he gently smoothes out.

It's the mental they'll be putting Girleen in before long if she carries on.

COLEMAN: Sure it's only a matter of time.

VALENE: Isn't that sad?

COLEMAN: Awful sad. *(Pause. Shrugging.)* Ah well.

He eats another vol-au-vent. VALENE *remembers something, fishes in the pockets of his jacket, takes out two ceramic figurines, places them on the shelf, uncaps his pen almost automatically, thinks better of marking them as before, and puts the pen away.*

I think I'm getting to like vol-au-vents now. I think I'm developing a taste for them. We ought to go to more funerals.

VALENE: They do have them at weddings too.

COLEMAN: Do they? Who'll next be getting married round here so? Girleen I would used to have said, as pretty as she is, only she'll probably have topped herself before ever she gets married.

VALENE: *Me* probably'll be the next one getting married, as handsome as I am. Did you see today all the young nuns eyeing me?

COLEMAN: Who'd go marrying you, sure? Even that no-lipped girl in Norway'd turn you down.

VALENE *(pause. Angrily)*: See, I'm stepping back now . . . I'm stepping back, like Father Walsh said and I'm forgiving ya, insulting me.

COLEMAN *(sincerely)*: Oh . . . oh, I'm sorry now, Valene. I'm sorry. It just slipped out on me without thinking.

VALENE: No harm done so, if only an accident it was.

COLEMAN: It *was* an accident. Although remember you did insult me there earlier, saying I was brain-damaged be stones as a gasur, and I didn't even pull you up on it.

VALENE: I apologise for saying you was brain-damaged as a gasur so.

COLEMAN: No apology was necessary, Valene, and I have saved you the last vol-au-venteen on top of it.

VALENE: You have that last vol-au-vent, Coleman. I'm not overly keen on vol-au-vents.

COLEMAN *nods in thanks and eats the vol-au-vent.*

VALENE: Weren't them young nuns lovely today now, Coleman?

COLEMAN: They was lovely nuns.

VALENE: They must've known Father Welsh from nun college or something.

COLEMAN: I'd like to touch them nuns both upstairs and downstairs, so I would. Except for the fat one on the end.

VALENE: She was a horror and she knew.

COLEMAN: If Dad was there today he'd've just gone screaming at them nuns.

VALENE: Why *did* Dad used to go screaming at nuns, Coleman?

COLEMAN: I don't have an idea at all why he used to scream at nuns. He must've had a bad experience with nuns as a child.

VALENE: If you hadn't blown the brains out of Dad we could ask him outright.

COLEMAN *stares at him sternly.*

VALENE: No, I'm not saying anything, now. I'm calm, I've stepped back, and I'm saying this quietly and without any spite at all, but you know well that that wasn't right, Coleman, shooting Dad in the head on us. In your heart anyways you know.

COLEMAN *(pause)*: I *do* know it wasn't right. Not only in me heart but in me head and in me everywhere. I was wrong for shooting Dad. I was dead wrong. And I'm sorry for it.

VALENE: And I'm sorry for sitting you down and making you sign your life away, Coleman. It was the only way at the time I could think of punishing ya. Well, I could've let you go to jail but I didn't want you going to jail and it wasn't out of miserliness that I stopped you going to jail. It was more out of I didn't want all on me own to be left here. I'd've missed ya. *(Pause.)* From this day on . . . from this day on, this house and everything in this house is half yours again, Coleman.

Touched, COLEMAN *offers his hand out and they shake, embarrassed. Pause.*

Is there any other confessions we have to get off our chests, now we're at it?

COLEMAN: There must be millions. *(Pause.)* Crushing your crisps to skitter, Valene, I'm sorry for.

VALENE: I forgive you for it. *(Pause.)* Do you remember that holiday in Lettermullen as gasurs we had, and you left your cowboy stagecoach out in the rain that night and next morning it was gone and Mam and Dad said 'Oh it must've been hijacked be Indians'. It wasn't hijacked be Indians. I'd got up early and pegged it in the sea.

COLEMAN (*pause*): I did love that cowboy stagecoach.

VALENE: I know you did, and I'm sorry for it.

COLEMAN (*pause*): That string of gob I dribbled on you on your birthday. I didn't try to suck it back up at all. I wanted it to hit your eye and I was glad. (*Pause.*) And I'm sorry for it.

VALENE: Okay. (*Pause.*) Maureen Folan did once ask me to ask you if you wanted to see a film at the Claddagh Palace with her, and she'd've driven ye and paid for dinner too, and from the tone of her voice it sounded like you'd've been on a promise after, but I never passed the message on to ya, out of nothing but pure spite.

COLEMAN: Sure that's no great loss, Valene. Maureen Folan looks like a thin-lipped ghost, with the hairstyle of a frightened red ape.

VALENE: But on a promise you'd've been.

COLEMAN: On a promise or no. That was nothing at all to go confessing. Okay, it's my go. I'm winning.

VALENE: What d'you mean, you're winning?

COLEMAN (*thinking*): Do you remember your Ker-Plunk game?

VALENE: I *do* remember me Ker-Plunk game.

COLEMAN: It wasn't Liam Hanlon stole all them marbles out of your Ker-Plunk game at all, it was me.

VALENE: What did you want me Ker-Plunk marbles for?

COLEMAN: I went slinging them at the swans in Galway. I had a great time.

VALENE: That ruined me Ker-Plunk. You can't play Ker-Plunk without marbles. And, sure, that was *both* of ours Ker-Plunk. That was just cutting off your nose to spite your face, Coleman.

COLEMAN: I know it was and I'm sorry, Valene. Your go now. (*Pause.*) You're too slow. D'you remember when we had them backward children staying for B & B, and they threw half your *Spiderman* comics in on the fire? They didn't. D'you know who did? I did. I only blamed them 'cos they were too daft to arg.

VALENE: They was good *Spiderman* comics, Coleman. Spiderman went fighting Doctor Octopus in them comics.

COLEMAN: And I'm sorry for it. Your go. (*Pause.*) You're too slow . . .

VALENE: Hey . . . !

COLEMAN: D'you remember when Pato Dooley beat the skitter out of you when he was twelve and you was twenty, and you never knew the reason why? I knew the reason why. I did tell him you'd called his dead mammy a hairy whore.

VALENE: With a fecking chisel that Pato Dooley beat me up that day! Almost had me fecking eye out!

COLEMAN: I think Pato must've liked his mammy or something. (*Pause.*) I'm awful sorry for it, Valene.

COLEMAN *burps lazily.*

VALENE: You do sound it!

COLEMAN: Shall I be having another go?

VALENE: I did pour a cup of piss in a pint of lager you drank one time, Coleman. Aye, and d'you know what, now? You couldn't even tell the differ.

COLEMAN (*pause*): When was this, now?

VALENE: When you was seventeen, this was. D'you remember that month you were laid up in hospital with bacterial tonsilitis? Around then it was. (*Pause.*) And I'm sorry for it, Coleman.

COLEMAN: I do take your poteen out its box each week, drink the half of it and fill the rest back up with water. Ten years this has been going on. You haven't tasted full-strength poteen since nineteen eighty-fecking-three.

VALENE (*drinks. Pause*): But you're sorry for it.

COLEMAN: I suppose I'm sorry for it, aye. (*Mumbling.*) Making me go drinking piss, and not just anybody's piss but *your* fecking piss . . .

VALENE (*angrily*): But you're sorry for it, you're saying?!

COLEMAN: I'm sorry for it, aye! I'm fecking sorry for it! Haven't I said?!

VALENE: That's okay, so, if you're sorry for it, although you don't sound fecking sorry for it.

COLEMAN: You can kiss me fecking arse so, Valene, if you don't . . . I'm taking a step back now, so I am. (*Pause.*) I'm sorry for watering your poteen down all these years, Valene. I am, now.

VALENE: Good-oh. *(Pause.)* Is it your go now or is it mine?

COLEMAN: I think it might be your go, Valene.

VALENE: Thank you, Coleman. D'you remember when Alison O'Hoolihan went sucking that pencil in the playground that time, and ye were to go dancing the next day, but somebody nudged that pencil and it got stuck in her tonsils on her, and be the time she got out of hospital she was engaged to the doctor who wrenched it out for her and wouldn't be giving you a fecking sniffeen. Do you remember, now?

COLEMAN: I do remember.

VALENE: That was me nudged that pencil, and it wasn't an accident at all. Pure jealous I was.

Pause. COLEMAN *throws his sausage rolls in* VALENE's *face and dives over the table for his neck.* VALENE *dodges the attack.*

And I'm sorry for it! I'm sorry for it! *(Pointing at letter.)* Father Welsh! Father Welsh!

VALENE *fends* COLEMAN *off. They stand staring at each other,* COLEMAN *seething.*

COLEMAN: Eh?!!

VALENE: Eh?

COLEMAN: I did fecking love Alison O'Hoolihan! We may've been married today if it hadn't been for that fecking pencil!

VALENE: What was she doing sucking it the pointy end inwards anyways? She was looking for trouble!

COLEMAN: And she fecking found it with you! That pencil could've killed Alison O'Hoolihan!

VALENE: And I'm sorry for it, I said. What are you doing pegging good sausage rolls at me? Them sausage rolls cost money. You were supposed to have taken a step back and went calming yourself, but you didn't, you just flew off the handle. Father Welsh's soul'll be roasting now because of you.

COLEMAN: Leave Father Welsh's soul out of it. This is about you sticking pencils down poor girls' gobs on them.

VALENE: That pencil is water under a bridge and I've apologised whole-hearted for that pencil. *(Sits down.)* And she had boss-eyes anyways.

COLEMAN: She didn't have boss-eyes! She had nice eyes!

VALENE: Well there was something funny about them.

COLEMAN: She had nice brown eyes.

VALENE: Oh aye. *(Pause.)* Well it's your go now, Coleman. Try and top that one for yourself. Heh.

COLEMAN: Try and top that one, is it?

VALENE: It is.

COLEMAN *thinks for a moment, smiles slightly, then sits back down.*

COLEMAN: I've taken a step back now.

VALENE: I can see you've taken a step back.

COLEMAN: I'm pure calm now. It does be good to get things off your chest.

VALENE: It *does* be good. I'm glad that pencil-nudging's off me chest. I can sleep nights now.

COLEMAN: Is it a relief to ya?

VALENE: It *is* a relief to me. *(Pause.)* What have you got cooking up?

COLEMAN: I have one and I'm terrible sorry for it. Oh terrible sorry I am.

VALENE: It won't be near as good as me pencilling poor boss-eyed Alison, whatever it is.

COLEMAN: Ah I suppose you're right, now. My one's only a weeny oul one. D'you remember you always thought it was Mairtin Hanlon snipped the ears off of poor Lassie, now?

VALENE *(confidently)*: I don't believe you at all. You're only making it up now, see.

COLEMAN: It wasn't wee Mairtin at all. D'you know who it was, now?

VALENE: Me arse was it you. You'll have to be doing better than that, now, Coleman.

COLEMAN: To the brookeen I dragged him, me scissors in hand, and him whimpering his fat gob off 'til the deed was done and he dropped down dead with not a fecking peep out of that whiny fecking dog.

VALENE: D'you see, it doesn't hurt me at all when you go making up lies. You don't understand the rules, Coleman. It does have to be true, else it's just plain daft. You can't go claiming credit for snipping the ears off a dog when you didn't lay a finger on that dog's ears, and the fecking world knows.

COLEMAN (*pause*): Is it evidence, so, you're after?

VALENE: It *is* evidence I'm after, aye. Go bring me evidence you did cut the ears off me dog. And be quick with that evidence.

COLEMAN: I won't be quick at all. I will take me time.

He slowly gets up and ambles to his room, closing its door behind him. VALENE *waits patiently, giving a worried laugh. After a ten-second pause,* COLEMAN *ambles back on, carrying a slightly wet brown paper bag. He pauses at the table a moment for dramatic effect, slowly opens the bag, pulls out a dog's big fluffy black ear, lays it on top of* VALENE's *head, takes out the second ear, pauses, places that on* VALENE's *head also, puts the empty bag down on the table, smoothes it out, then sits down in the armchair left.* VALENE *has been staring out into space all the while, dumbstruck. He tilts his head so that the ears fall down onto the table, and he stares at them a while.* COLEMAN *picks up* VALENE's *felt-tip pen, brings it over and lays it on the table.*

COLEMAN: There's your little pen, now, Val. Why don't you mark them dog's ears with your V, so we'll be remembering who they belong to.

He sits back down in the armchair.

And do you want to hear something else, Valene? I'm sorry for cutting off them dog's ears. With all me fecking heart I'm sorry, oh aye, because I've tooken a step back now, look at me . . .

He half-laughs through his nose. VALENE *gets up, stares blankly at* COLEMAN *a moment, goes to the cupboard right and, with his back to* COLEMAN, *pulls the butcher's knife out of it. In the same brief second* COLEMAN *stands, pulls the shotgun down from above the stove and sits down with it.* VALENE *turns, knife ready. The gun is pointed directly at him.* VALENE *wilts slightly, thinks about it a moment, regains his courage and his anger, and slowly approaches* COLEMAN, *raising the knife.*

COLEMAN (*surprised, slightly scared*): What are you doing now, Valene?

VALENE (*blankly*): Oh not a thing am I doing, Coleman, other than killing ya.

COLEMAN: Be putting that knife back in that drawer, you.

VALENE: No, I'll be putting it in the head of you, now.

COLEMAN: Don't you see me gun?

VALENE: Me poor fecking Lassie, who never hurt a flea.

VALENE has gotten all the way up to COLEMAN, *so that the barrel of the gun is touching his chest. He raises the knife to its highest point.*

COLEMAN: What are you doing, now? Stop it.

VALENE: I'll stop it, all right . . .

COLEMAN: Father Welsh's soul, Valene. Father Wel—

VALENE: Father Welsh's soul me fecking arse! Father Welsh's soul didn't come into play when you hacked me dog's ears off him and kept them in a bag!

COLEMAN: Ar that was a year ago. How does that apply?

VALENE: Be saying goodbye to the world, you, ya feck!

COLEMAN: *You'll* have to be saying goodbye to the world too, so, because I'll be bringing you with me.

VALENE: Do I look like I mind that at all, now?

COLEMAN *(pause)*: Er er, wait wait wait, now . . .

VALENE: Wha . . . ?

COLEMAN: Look at me gun. Look at me gun where it's going, do ya see . . . ?

COLEMAN *slides the gun away and down from* VALENE'S *chest 'til it points directly at the door of the stove.*

VALENE *(pause)*: Be pointing that gun away from me stove, now.

COLEMAN: I won't be. Stab away, now. It's your stove it'll be'll be going with me instead of ya.

VALENE: Leave . . . what . . . ? That was a three-hundred-pound stove now, Coleman . . .

COLEMAN: I know well it was.

VALENE: Be leaving it alone. That's just being sly, that is.

COLEMAN: Be backing off you with that knife, you sissy-arse.

VALENE *(tearfully)*: You're not a man at all, pointing guns at stoves.

COLEMAN: I don't care if I am or I'm not. Be backing off, I said.

VALENE: You're just a . . . you're just a . . .

COLEMAN: Eh?

VALENE: Eh?

COLEMAN: Eh?

VALENE: You're not a man at all, you.

COLEMAN: Be backing away now, you cry-baby. Be taking a step back for yourself. Eheh.

VALENE: *(pause)*: I'm backing away now, so I am.

COLEMAN: That'd be the best thing aye.

VALENE *slowly retreats, lays the knife on the table and sits down there sadly, gently stroking his dog's ears.* COLEMAN *is still pointing the gun at the stove door. He shakes his head slightly.*

COLEMAN: I can't believe you raised a knife to me. No, I can't believe you raised a knife to your own brother.

VALENE: You raised a knife to me own dog and raised a gun to our own father, did a lot more damage than a fecking knife, now.

COLEMAN: No, I can't believe it. I can't believe you raised a knife to me.

VALENE: Stop going on about raising a knife, and be pointing that gun away from me fecking stove, now, in case it does go off be accident.

COLEMAN: Be accident, is it?

VALENE: Is the safety catch on that gun, now?

COLEMAN: The safety catch, is it?

VALENE: Aye, the safety catch! The safety catch! Is it ten million times I have to be repeating meself?

COLEMAN: The safety catch, uh-huh . . .

He jumps to his feet, points the gun down at the stove and fires, blowing the right-hand side apart. VALENE falls to his knees in horror, his face in his hands. COLEMAN cocks the gun again and blows the left-hand side apart also, then nonchalantly sits back down.

No, the safety catch isn't on at all, Valene. Would you believe it?

Pause. VALENE is still kneeling there, dumbstruck.

And I'll tell you another thing . . .

He suddenly jumps up again and, holding the shotgun by the barrel, starts smashing it violently into the figurines, shattering them to pieces and sending them flying around the room until not a single one remains standing. VALENE screams throughout. After COLEMAN has finished he sits again, the gun across his lap. VALENE is still kneeling. Pause.

And don't go making out that you didn't deserve it, because we both know full well that you did.

VALENE *(numbly)*: You've broken all me figurines, Coleman.

COLEMAN: I have. Did you see me?

VALENE: And you've blown me stove to buggery.

COLEMAN: This is a great gun for blowing holes in things.

VALENE (*standing*): And now you do have no bullets left in that great gun.

He lazily picks the knife back up and approaches COLE-MAN. *But as he does so* COLEMAN *opens the barrel of the gun, tosses away the spent cartridges, fishes in his pocket, comes out with a clenched fist that may or may not contain another cartridge, and loads, or pretends to load, the bullet into the gun, without* VALENE *or the audience at any time knowing if there is a bullet or not.* COLEMAN *snaps the barrel shut and lazily points it at* VALENE'S *head.*

There was no bullet in that hand, Coleman! No bullet at all!

COLEMAN: Maybe there wasn't, now. Maybe it's pretending I am. Be taking a pop for yourself.

VALENE: I *will* be taking a pop for meself.

COLEMAN: And then we'll see.

Long, long pause.

VALENE: I want to kill you, Coleman.

COLEMAN: Ar, don't be saying that, now, Val.

VALENE (*sadly*): It's true, Coleman. I want to kill you.

COLEMAN (*pause*): Try so.

Coleman cocks the gun. Pause. VALENE *turns the knife around and around in his hand, staring at* COLEMAN *all the while, until his head finally droops and he returns the knife to the drawer.* COLEMAN *uncocks the gun, stands, and lays it down on the table, staying near it.* VALENE *idles to the stove and touches the letter pinned above it.*

VALENE: Father Welsh is burning in hell, now, because of our fighting.

COLEMAN: Well did we ask him to go betting his soul on us? No. And, sure, it's pure against the rules for priests to go betting anyways, neverminding with them kinds of stakes. Sure a fiver would've been overdoing it on us, let alone his soul. And what's wrong with fighting anyways? I do like a good fight. It does show you care, fighting does. That's what oul sissy Welsh doesn't understand. Don't you like a good fight?

VALENE: I *do* like a good fight, the same as that. Although I don't like having me dog murdered on me, and me fecking dad murdered on me.

COLEMAN: And I'm sorry for your dog and Dad, Valene. I *am* sorry. Truly I'm sorry. And nothing to do with Father Welsh's letter is this at all. From me own heart this is. The same goes for your stove and your poor figurines too. Look at them. That was pure temper, that was. Although, admit it, you asked for that stove and them figurines.

VALENE: You never fecking stop, you. *(Pause.) Are* you sorry, Coleman?

COLEMAN: I am, Valene.

VALENE *(pause)*: Maybe Father Walsh's Welsh's soul'll be all right so.

COLEMAN: Maybe it will, now. Maybe it will.

VALENE: He wasn't such a bad fella.

COLEMAN: He wasn't.

VALENE: He wasn't a great fella, but he wasn't a bad fella.

COLEMAN: Aye. *(Pause.)* He was a *middling* fella.

VALENE: He was a *middling* fella.

COLEMAN *(pause)*: I'm going out for a drink for meself. Will you be coming with me?

VALENE: Aye, in a minute now I'll come.

COLEMAN *goes to the front door.* VALENE *looks over the smashed figurines sadly.*

COLEMAN: I'll help you be clearing your figurines up when I get back, Valene. Maybe we can glue some of them together. Do you still have your superglue?

VALENE: I do have me superglue, although I think the top's gone hard.

COLEMAN: Aye, that's the trouble with superglue.

VALENE: Ah, the house insurance'll cover me figurines anyways. As well as me stove.

COLEMAN: Oh . . .

VALENE *(pause)*: What, 'oh?'

COLEMAN: Do you remember a couple of weeks ago there when you asked me did I go stealing your insurance money and I said no, I paid it in for you?

VALENE: I do remember.

COLEMAN: *(pause)*: I didn't pay it in at all. I pocketed the lot of it, pissed it up a wall.

VALENE, seething, darts for the gun. COLEMAN dashes out through the front door. VALENE brings the gun to the door and chases out, but COLEMAN is long gone. VALENE returns a few seconds later, gun in hand, shaking with rage, almost in tears. After a while he begins to calm down, taking deep breaths. He looks down at the gun in his hands a moment, then gently opens the barrel to see if COLEMAN had really loaded it earlier. He had. VALENE takes the cartridge out.

VALENE: He'd've fecking shot me too. He'd've shot his own fecking brother! On top of his dad! On top of me stove!

He tosses the gun and cartridge away, rips FATHER WELSH's letter off the cross, knocking GIRLEEN's chain onto the floor, brings the letter back to the table and takes out a box of matches.

And you, you whiny fecking priest. Do I need your soul hovering o'er me the rest of me fecking life? How could anybody be getting on with that feck?

He strikes a match and lights the letter, which he glances over as he holds up. After a couple of seconds, the letter barely singed, VALENE blows the flames out and looks at it on the table, sighing.

(Quietly.) I'm too fecking kind-hearted is my fecking trouble.

He returns to the cross and pins the chain and letter back onto it, smoothing the letter out. He puts on his jacket, checks it for loose change and goes to the front door.

Well I won't be buying the fecker a pint anyways. I'll tell you that for nothing, Father Welsh Walsh Welsh.

VALENE *glances back at the letter a second, sadly, looks down at the floor, then exits. Lights fade, with one light lingering on the crucifix and letter a half second longer than the others.*